"How about giving me some parenting lessons?"

Derrick's handsome face flushed and Anna found it an extremely appealing sight.

"You see," he said, "I'm single. I've spent a fraction of my time around children. So what do I say to this boy who's suddenly become my son? What do I do?"

Anna knew he was still speaking, but she wasn't really listening. She'd stopped focusing on the conversation when he'd said the word *single*.

The fact that she had responded so strongly to his pronouncement should have triggered warning bells inside her head. But it hadn't.

"So, how about it?" he asked.

"But I'm no parent." As Anna said the words, her heart fluttered in her chest painfully. This man would never know how it hurt to reveal that fact.

Dear Reader,

In 1993 beloved, bestselling author Diana Palmer launched the FABULOUS FATHERS series with *Emmett* (SR#910), which was her 50th Silhouette book. Readers fell in love with that Long, Tall Texan who discovered the meaning of love and fatherhood, and ever since, the FABULOUS FATHERS series has been a favorite. And now, to celebrate the publication of the *50th* FABULOUS FATHERS book, Silhouette Romance is very proud to present a brand-new novel by Diana Palmer, *Mystery Man*, and Fabulous Father Canton Rourke.

Silhouette Romance is just chock-full of special books this month! We've got *Miss Maxwell Becomes a Mom*, book one of Donna Clayton's new miniseries, THE SINGLE DADDY CLUB. And Alice Sharpe's *Missing: One Bride* is book one of our SURPRISE BRIDES trio, three irresistible books by three wonderful authors about very unusual wedding situations.

Rounding out the month is Jodi O'Donnell's newest title, *Real Marriage Material*, in which a sexy man of the land gets tamed. Robin Wells's *Husband and Wife...Again* tells the tale of a divorced couple reuniting in a delightful way. And finally, in *Daddy for Hire* by Joey Light, a hunk of a man becomes the most muscular nanny there ever was, all for love of his little girl.

Enjoy Diana Palmer's *Mystery Man* and all of our wonderful books this month. There's just no better way to start off springtime than with six books bursting with love!

Regards,

Melissa Senate
Senior Editor
Silhouette Books

Please address questions and book requests to:
Silhouette Reader Service
U.S.: 3010 Walden Ave., P.O. Box 1325, Buffalo, NY 14269
Canadian: P.O. Box 609, Fort Erie, Ont. L2A 5X3

MISS MAXWELL BECOMES A MOM

Donna Clayton

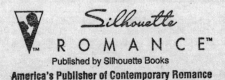

Silhouette

ROMANCE™

Published by Silhouette Books

America's Publisher of Contemporary Romance

For my courageous friend
Karen Richmond
with love

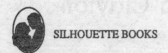 SILHOUETTE BOOKS

ISBN 0-373-19211-8

MISS MAXWELL BECOMES A MOM

DONNA CLAYTON

is proud to be a recipient of the HOLT Medallion, an award honoring outstanding literary talent. And seeing her work appear on the Waldenbooks Series Bestsellers List has given her a great deal of joy and satisfaction.

Reading is one of Donna's favorite ways to while away a rainy afternoon. She loves to hike, too. Another hobby added to her list of fun things to do is traveling. She fell in love with Europe during her first trip abroad recently and plans to return often. Oh, and Donna still collects cookbooks, but as her writing career grows, she finds herself using them less and less.

**THE SINGLE DADDY CLUB
DECLARATION**

We, the undersigned, do solemnly swear
to uphold the standards of the
Single Daddy Club. We shall be loving,
nurturing parents—proud of our single
status. Although female companionship
would be nice, we shall never be convinced
to enter into the state of matrimony solely
for the sake of our children.
(We shall, however, be happy to settle
down with the woman of our dreams…
if she ever shows up!)

Fatherhood forever!

Derrick Cheney

Reese Newton

Jason Devlin

Chapter One

Derrick turned off the engine of his car and glanced at his watch. He had exactly four minutes before his parent-teacher conference, so he unlatched his seat belt and took the note from his inside jacket pocket. He studied the fluid, elegant handwriting once again.

Behavior problem. The words seemed to jump right out at him. The very idea had Derrick frowning with bewilderment. Timmy was such a quiet, unassuming child. Derrick found it hard to imagine that his six-year-old godson could have a behavior problem.

But then, Timmy had only been living with him for the past ten months, and Derrick had been preoccupied with the red tape involved in resigning his commission in the Navy, and then the task of opening his own accounting business had kept him busy.

Guilt crept across Derrick's skin with the light touch of a horde of frantic spiders. He should be spending more time with Timmy, he knew that deep down in his heart. But the tough decision of letting his military career go, the difficulty in convincing his superiors that resigning his commission was the right move for him and the many hours he'd spent beating the pavement as a civilian to build a firm foundation for his new business were all necessary steps toward giving Timmy the kind of stable home Derrick was determined the child should have. The kind of stable home he certainly hadn't had during the first six years of his life.

Knowing the unsettled existence his godson had experienced, Derrick realized that he probably should have met with Timmy's first grade teacher prior to the opening of school; he probably should have explained the boy's unusual situation to the woman. But he'd been so damned busy. He'd barely gotten Timmy enrolled in the school by the deadline, and before Derrick had realized it, the big, yellow bus had been honking outside the house.

For a rare instant he felt his mind drifting as he wondered what type of teacher this Miss Maxwell was. He hoped she wasn't as flighty in person as she'd sounded on the phone when he'd called to make an appointment to see her. As he drew in a deep sigh, Derrick's eyes were once again drawn to the notepaper that was shaped like a huge apple.

Special Education classes. The well-formed penmanship shaped the phrase into delicate curls, but that didn't stop the words from causing an icy shudder to course the length of Derrick's spine.

In his youth Derrick had attended a crowded public school. And he knew that the Special Ed. class was made up of misbehaving misfits, students who refused to follow rules and regulations. Teachers didn't want these malcontents in their classrooms, so semester to semester, year to year, the students were never assimilated back into the normal system. They were pigeon-holed. Stymied by a label.

He remembered befriending a few of those kids who had been relegated to Special Ed. Once those boys had that dreaded mark on their records, they lived with it for the remainder of their school days. Hell, some of them lived with it for the rest of their lives!

Derrick would never permit that to happen to Timmy. Not after the chaotic life he'd had, not after the heartache he'd experienced from losing his father. Derrick refused to stand by and let anyone—including this Miss Maxwell—do anything to hurt Timmy.

The repeated beep, beep of his wristwatch alarm alerted Derrick that it was time for his meeting with Timmy's teacher. Automatically he pushed the tiny button that reset the alarm, then he neatly folded the note and replaced it in his jacket pocket. As he opened the car door, he couldn't help the worried frown that planted itself deep in his brow. This father business was so very new to him, he really didn't know what to expect. He strode across the parking lot toward the entrance of the school, trying to push his concern aside. But the anxiety he felt refused to be conquered by sheer force of will.

Look, he silently lectured himself as he grasped the handle of the heavy door, all you need to do is keep Timmy's best interests at heart.

The office was dark and empty, and Derrick looked up and down the hallway as he jingled the loose change in his trouser pocket. He was certain he'd arranged to meet Timmy's teacher right here. His sigh was ragged with irritation. There was nothing for him to do but wait for the woman.

Five slow, tedious minutes passed. Then six. Seven. Eight.

Derrick felt his irritation rev into second gear, then third. If there was one thing he hated, it was wasting time waiting for people. It was time to take matters into his own hands.

He followed the short hallway into the school until he came to a Y in the corridor. Although there had been several cars in the parking lot, the building seemed completely deserted. He took the hallway to the left, hoping it would lead to the first grade classrooms.

The first room he came to was dark and vacant. He was pleased to see a nameplate stating Grade One— Classroom One, however, the pleasure he felt was like a tiny spritz of cool mist that immediately evaporated when it came into contact with the embers of annoyance that glowed inside him like hot coals.

As he moved further on down the corridor, he ran agitated fingers through his dark hair. He'd just talked to the woman yesterday afternoon. How could she possibly have forgotten their appointment?

Then he saw light and the soft, muffled sounds of movement coming from the room farthest down the hall.

"Bingo," he whispered.

He stopped in the doorway and blinked. The room seemed alive with a profusion of color and movement. It was in direct contrast with the drab gray paint of the walls of the hallway. The large, tempera-painted leaves suspended from the ceiling twirled slowly on their string tethers. More larger-than-life autumn leaves were plastered to the windows. These were made of tissue paper causing the late-afternoon sunlight to glint in garish rainbow hues.

One corner of the room was obviously a play area, and Derrick was surprised at how the books, games and blocks were in such disarray.

"Mr. Cheney."

Derrick swiveled his attention and his gaze in the direction of the soft, feminine voice that called his name.

The slim, petite woman was standing in front of the bulletin board on a small, child-sized chair. The stapler clutched in her slender hand was folded open, and she was evidently using it to secure bold, blue cutout letters to the board. But what Derrick noticed above all else was the fact that her clothing was as colorful, maybe even more so, than the classroom itself.

The filmy, sheer material of her turquoise skirt was very full and hung nearly to her ankles. His brain registered an underskirt of some dense, dark fabric. The sash gathered around her trim waist was purple, her simple cotton pullover was bright red. A draping of purple glass beads hung from her neck and her small, dainty ears. And when her arm dropped to her side, Derrick heard the tinkle of numerous colorfully enameled bangle bracelets.

He'd taken so long simply gazing at her in silence that when he finally did lift his eyes to her face he felt…embarrassed. But he immediately forgot his chagrin as he became lost in her eyes. They were a piercing green. And interesting. Filled with merriment. Her full mouth was drawn into a small smile. She reached up with her empty hand and plunged her fingers into the mass of her full, multilayered hair that was so black and shiny it gleamed blue in the light.

"Please come in."

Hearing her soft, pleasant voice for the second time seemed to knock him out of his stuporous trance.

She stepped down from the chair, placed the stapler on her desk, and walked toward him.

"You are Timmy Cheney's father?" she asked. "I'm Miss Maxwell."

"Actually...I'm...um..." He let the words trail. Why couldn't he find his tongue? Or collect his thoughts? He reached out instinctively, took her hand and shook it. Her skin was warm and silky smooth.

Miss Maxwell's laughter was light, like the tinkling of far-off bells. It seemed to echo inside his head, making him feel strange, as though he were grinning like a fool, yet he knew for a fact there was no smile on his face.

"It's okay," she said. "There's no need to be disconcerted. Your reaction is quite normal. My appearance can be somewhat...overwhelming to some people. Most people, actually."

Again he heard that tinkling laughter.

"Mr. Styes, our principal," she continued, "hates the way I dress. But as the great Perry Como says, 'I gotta be me.'"

Her brow furrowed with the most adorable frown. "Or was that Frank Sinatra?"

What the hell is the woman talking about? his hazy brain questioned. More importantly, what the hell is the matter with *me?*

He was normally competent, precise, articulate. But standing there in front of Timmy's first grade teacher, Derrick was finding his thoughts flying in utter confusion, his tongue tied up in knots. He felt an overwhelming need to offer an excuse for this strange, yet wholly perplexing fog he found himself smothered in. But how could he offer anything? Especially when he could come up with no justifiable reason for his lame behavior for himself, let alone for her.

After what felt like an eon of awkward silence, he found himself murmuring, "Sorry."

"Oh—" she airily waved aside his apology "—don't feel bad about being late."

Derrick watched her turn and walk to her desk. Her filmy turquoise skirt clung to the slight swell of her hips as they dipped and swayed from side to side. His eyes were glued to the woman's cute derriere, and the sight threatened to suck him even deeper into the whirling vortex of stupefaction that was spinning around and around him. But something about what she'd said tugged violently at his subconscious, something she'd said parted the clouds in his brain.

"I used the time wisely," she told him, "to put up a new bulletin board."

"What did you say?" he asked.

She was facing him once again, and with the sight of her shapely rear end taken from his view, sanity returned more quickly.

"I said I put the time to good use," she repeated for him. "I put up a bulletin—"

"No, no," he said, his tone short. "Before that."

She hesitated a moment, that cute little frown furrowing her brow again.

"Well, I don't remember my exact words," she said. "But I think I told you not to worry about being late for our meeting."

"That's what I thought you said." Derrick nodded as his mental acuity returned. He felt more clearheaded than he had in many moments. Along with the restoration of crystal coherence came the strong annoyance he'd been feeling toward this woman—an annoyance that was fast building into full-fledged indignation.

"Miss Maxwell, I certainly do beg your pardon—" he placed sarcastic emphasis on the last three words "—but *I* was not late."

Delicate, dark eyelashes fluttered up and down as she blinked several times.

"And," he added, "not only did I arrive on time, but I also arrived at our appointed meeting place. The school office."

Instinctively she looked up at the large-faced clock on her classroom wall. Then her green gaze darted back to his face.

"Are you certain we arranged to meet at the office?"

"Absolutely," he said with great satisfaction.

"Oh."

That one tiny word came out all breathy, and her lips formed around it in a soft, luscious circle. He felt his palms grow moist and he fought the urge to tug at his shirt collar.

Derrick's inhalation was sharp as he averted his gaze to the floor. What in the world was wrong with him? He was furious now. But for the life of him, he couldn't say whether he was more irritated at Miss Maxwell...or himself.

"Is that all you have to say?" He could feel his face flushing with heated annoyance.

Her head tilted to one side. "You're angry," she observed softly.

Derrick felt the tremendous momentum of his emotions skid to a halt, or at least to a slow crawl. He'd expected an apology from her, or at least an explanation of some kind. He hadn't expected her to confront

him with what he was feeling. The fact that she had
done so made him feel...almost silly. Like he should
never have become upset with the situation in the first
place.

She gave the clock another glance. "We're only ten
minutes late," she said. "Let's sit down and talk about
Timmy."

Her buoyant tone of voice irritated the hell out of
him all over again. It was as though she thought he
was blowing this whole thing out of proportion. Yet at
the same time he felt an overwhelming urge to apologize for feeling irritated in the first place. This woman
had his feelings all twisted up in complicated knots.

Still, he dug in his heels. She was the one who was
late, and not only that, she hadn't even come to the
arranged meeting place. Ten minutes, indeed.

"It's been twelve minutes," he found himself saying. "Nearly thirteen. And do you have any idea what
a person can accomplish in thirteen minutes?"

Anna Maxwell took a moment to gather her
thoughts. This was one uptight man standing in front
of her. He seemed determined to argue about something she felt didn't need arguing.

The look in his eye. The set of his jaw. The tight
pitch of his voice. He was obviously angry that she
hadn't met him at the office. She really didn't remember arranging to meet him there—although that wasn't
out of the realm of possibility. Sometimes little details
such as that seemed to get away from her. That's why
she made lists. Lots of lists....

She smiled, hoping to dispel some of the tension that
enveloped the two of them. Why was he so hung up
on a measly thirteen minutes?

"Well..." She hesitated. "I nearly finished my bulletin board while I waited here for you."

Her words only seemed to ruffle him further.

"But the whole point is," he stressed, "you shouldn't have been waiting for me *here*."

Her brows rose slightly. "I understand your point, Mr. Cheney. And I am sorry."

His reaction to her apology was astonishing to her. He looked as though he couldn't decide whether to be smug that he'd proven his point, or chagrined because he'd pushed the issue too far. The indecision on his face almost made her chuckle, but she thought it wise not to.

"Please," she said softly, "let's sit down."

She kept an extra adult-sized, straight-backed chair in the room, and she offered it to him. Many parents didn't feel comfortable sitting on the tiny, wooden chairs that the children used, and she sensed Timmy's father would have a hard time fitting his tall frame onto one.

"As I said in my note," she began, "Timmy is having some behavior problems."

"I read your note. But I must let you know right up front that I'll never allow you to place Timmy in a Special Education class."

Anna frowned. "But why? Don't you want Timmy to get the special attention he needs?"

"Special attention?"

The sarcasm in his tone and the skepticism on his face bewildered Anna.

"Yes," she said. "I think your son needs some extra attention—"

He interrupted her with his upraised hand. "Tim isn't my son," he told her quietly.

His whole demeanor seemed to alter, Anna noticed, with this sudden change of topic. Where his expression before was filled with exasperation and anxiety, his features were now fixed with a somberness that had her leaning forward a fraction.

She had to admit, his statement surprised her. She had the distinct urge to flip open Timmy Cheney's file and reread its contents. But she could tell from the tone of voice used by the man sitting in front of her, from the set of his body, that he had a story to tell. A story that was filled with sadness, her gut instinct told her, one that would tell her much more about Timmy than any file folder would.

Resting her elbows on her desktop, she said, "He isn't?"

Mr. Cheney shook his head slowly from side to side, and she couldn't help but notice how the sharp angles of his face, matched with the strength of his jaw, made for a very pleasing combination. Mr. Cheney was an extremely handsome man.

"No. You see, Timmy's father, James, was my cousin." He stopped a moment to clear his throat. "James and I were both military men."

Anna noticed how he'd used the past tense verb to describe both himself and his cousin. Whatever had happened to Timmy's father, she knew the incident had changed many lives.

"James was killed ten months ago in a routine training drill—a stupid mistake that caused the death of three men."

The tightness in his voice, the sudden tenseness in his face, made her heart constrict with sympathy.

"I was Timmy's godfather," he went on. "I was also named as his guardian."

"Where's Timmy's mother?" The question was spoken before Anna could stop herself.

"She died when Timmy was just a baby."

His gaze slid away from hers, and Anna had the feeling that he was reluctant, maybe even embarrassed to explain the circumstances surrounding the woman's death.

"She was drinking and driving, you see," he said. "The only good thing about the situation—if there can be a good thing—is that she had the accident *before* picking Timmy up at the sitter's."

A shiver coursed across Anna's skin. "She was on her way to pick up Timmy?"

He nodded, his piercing eyes directly on hers now.

"And she'd been drinking?"

Again he nodded silently. Then he said, "Being a Navy wife can be lonely. Tina took solace in alcohol. It was but for the grace of God that she didn't take Timmy with her."

How could any woman do such a thing? Anna wondered. If she had been bestowed with the miraculous gift of a baby, she would never, ever…

She let the thought trail. She would never, ever find herself in anything remotely resembling those circumstances. She knew she would never, ever be given the miraculous gift of—

Anna shoved the painful idea from her and focused on the man who sat in front of her.

"Timmy's had it pretty rough." She said the words gently, hoping to convey the message that she understood Timmy a little more from what he was telling her.

"You could say that." He ran his fingers through his sandy blond hair. "You see, James's job entailed quite a bit of travel. He was stationed on ships for weeks at a time. Of course, he couldn't take his son, so Timmy would stay with one family or another. Whoever was willing to take him in. Timmy stayed with me for a couple of months once when James and I happened to be stationed at the same base and he pulled a stint out at sea."

That poor child, Anna thought. Shuffled from house to house. No wonder he was behaving badly. Timmy was screaming for attention.

"I tried to tell James that he needed to leave the service," he continued. "I tried to tell him that this was no sort of life for Timmy. But he wouldn't listen. And he loved being an officer too much to give it up."

The bracelets around her wrist jangled as she raised her hand to tuck her hair behind her ear. "I have to agree," she told him. "It sounds like Timmy was in a bad situation."

"Don't get me wrong," he said. "James loved his son. He just...loved the Navy more."

Anna felt her insides quake. She couldn't help feeling resentful and angry at people like Timmy's parents. They had been given a precious child and they hadn't appreciated him.

"It's so sad." There was a huge measure of sorrow in her whispered statement.

"But I'm trying to change all that," he said. Again he ran his fingers through his short, blond hair. "I've resigned my active commission, I've bought a house here in Bayview and I'm starting my own accounting firm. I was talked into retaining a reserve status, but if that presents any kind of problem with Tim—*any* kind of problem—then I'll give that up, too."

She looked at him for a moment. "You're changing your whole life...for Timmy."

His chin rose just a fraction, and Anna could tell that he'd defended his decision before. Probably to his superiors in the Navy when he'd retired—no, she silently corrected, he'd *resigned* his full-time status and joined the Naval Reserves.

"Timmy deserves a settled childhood," he told her. "Lord knows he hasn't had one up until now."

Hearing all that this man was giving up made Anna's heart soften toward him. He was changing his life for Timmy—making great sacrifices for his godson.

There was a moment of easy silence during which Anna remembered the reason they were both here— Timmy's behavior problem. And as much as she hated to do it, she felt it necessary to get them back on track.

"With all that Timmy's been through in his life," she began, "don't you think he could use a little special attention?"

His dark eyes narrowed. "We're back to the Special Ed. thing again."

"I—"

"I realize teachers don't like to deal with problem students," he stated. "If you've decided you don't like Timmy, then I can have him placed in another first-grade class."

Anna's mouth actually dropped open. Never, in all her years as a primary school teacher, had she ever been accused of not liking one of her students. And she couldn't believe how his accusation hurt her feelings. She fought to control the emotions churning inside her chest. It was hard to breathe, and she dragged oxygen around the huge lump that had formed in her throat.

"I love Timmy," she said weakly. "I love all my students."

But she knew he hadn't heard her when he barreled forward.

"I'll never agree to placing Timmy in a special class," he said, his voice rising. "I won't let you label him. I won't let you blacken his record and ruin the rest of his school years." He leaned toward her. "He's just starting out. If you place him in any kind of special class, he'll never get out."

Suddenly she understood what he was thinking and she took a deep breath. Weaving her fingers together, she placed her hands on top of Timmy's folder.

"I'm not certain you understand the concept of Special Education," she gently told him.

"I understand perfectly," he stated. "You take him out of a normal class, with normal kids, and Timmy starts believing he's not normal."

"That's silly," she said. "Special Ed. isn't what it was twenty or twenty-five years ago when you were in school."

"And that's exactly what I'd expect to hear from a teacher representing this school system."

Patience, she told herself.

"You really don't understand, Mr. Cheney..."

"And I don't care to understand, Miss Maxwell. Because I'm not going to agree to the idea."

She watched him straighten suddenly.

"Sending Timmy to another class will accomplish one thing," he said. "And that's taking the problem off your hands."

She cocked her head to one side. "Are you actually implying that I'm taking the easy road here?"

"I'm simply making an observation."

"Mr. Cheney—"

"If you send Timmy somewhere else, he'll still have a problem." He sat back, crossing his arms over his chest. "And you won't."

Anna couldn't believe what she was hearing. "Of course I will," she said. "I'll still have a problem, because Timmy will still be my student. I care about Timmy. And it upsets me terribly that you think I want to foist him and his problem off on someone else, because—"

"Then don't."

Swift and all-consuming anger crowded out all logical thought. She'd only meant to suggest that Timmy spend two half-hour sessions a week with the school counselor—sessions that would fall under the jurisdiction of the Special Ed. department of the school system. But this infuriating man wouldn't let her explain that. He had it in his head that she was going to send him off to Siberia or something. She pressed her lips together and felt her blood boil.

Anna was silent for a moment as she dealt with this unnatural emotion. She never got angry. Well, only on very rare occasions. But she was hopping mad right now.

"Mr. Cheney—" her calm, quiet tone belied the magnitude of insult she was feeling, but before she could speak her mind, he stopped her with an upraised palm.

"Look," he said, "all I'm asking is that you give the boy some time. You've barely had him in your class a month. How can you get to know a child in that short a time?"

She clamped her lips shut, thinking it best to get her

anger under control and hear him out before she commented.

He cupped his kneecap with his palm. "I know I can do this," he said. "I know I'm capable of giving Timmy the stable, happy home he deserves."

There was something in his tone that told Anna he really wasn't quite certain he was telling the truth. But the determined set of his jaw revealed to her that he'd never in a million years admit it out loud.

"I just need some time," he went on. "And a little help."

She stared at him long and hard.

"So," she said finally, "you insult me in one breath and ask for my help in another."

The look on his handsome face was one she would never forget—a subtle mixture of charming, boyish grin and good-hearted apology. Surprisingly the expression melted away every nuance of anger she'd been feeling. In fact, she had to work at not smiling at him in response.

"Okay, Mr. Cheney." She knew the warmhearted surrender she was feeling was showing in her eyes, even though she fought to keep her lips from quirking upward. "What did you have in mind?"

He raised one hand. "I don't know, really. I mean, I *know* I can do this—"

Again she heard the tiniest quiver of doubt in his voice.

"But..." He let the sentence trail.

Anna sat quietly, allowing the silence to linger between them. She wanted to be certain he had no suggestions for solutions before she began handing out advice.

When it was evident to her that he was waiting for

her to speak, she said, "I think Timmy needs rules."
She brushed a long, curling lock of her hair back over
her shoulder. "He refuses to follow the most funda-
mental rules of courtesy. He snatches toys, books, puz-
zles—whatever it is he wants—from the other children.
It's as though 'thank you' and 'please' aren't part of
his vocabulary."

She stopped when she saw him frown.

"But that doesn't sound like Timmy," he said. "Of
course, he seems to stay in his room quite a bit, but
when we're together, he's terribly quiet, terribly polite."

Bewilderment knit her brow as a realization struck
her. "You know," she said, "Timmy's very polite to
me, too." She lightly tapped her chin with the knuckle
of her index finger. "Do you suppose…?" Then she
focused again on Timmy's godfather. "How much exposure has he had to other children?"

He shrugged. "I know he'd been bounced around
from one couple to another when he was living on base
and his father was away. Most of them were elderly
couples, one or two might have had children in high
school…I really don't know. For the most part, though,
I think it's been just Timmy and James."

Anna nodded slowly. "It could be that the poor child
doesn't know how to act with other children." She
gazed off, deep in thought. Ideas were forming in her
head, fast and furious.

"Okay," she said finally, "I'm going to impose
some rules of discipline on the entire class. That way
Timmy won't feel singled out. I can discuss with the
children the need to be responsible for your own actions." She nodded her head, liking the thought more

and more as it developed. "The whole class can benefit from this."

Mr. Cheney's golden brown eyes locked onto hers, and she knew he had something he wanted to say.

"That's great," he told her. "I think some strict rules will be great for Timmy." He swallowed. Licked his lips. Reached up and tugged on his earlobe.

Suddenly she chuckled. "Why is it I hear a big *but* in there somewhere?"

One corner of his wide mouth tilted up in a soft grin.

"All of that sounds great for Timmy—" his grin widened "—but I have to admit…I was looking for some help…for me."

Her hand lowered to the desktop almost of its own volition. "For you?"

His handsome face flushed, and Anna found it an extremely appealing sight. It was odd that she found his difficult predicament so…enchanting.

But then, maybe it wasn't his predicament that she found enchanting…maybe it was the fact that he—this attractive, capable man—was asking for her help in the situation.

"Yeah, well," he began.

He glanced off for a moment, and when he looked at her again, the intensity in his dark gaze held her mesmerized.

"You see," he said, "I'm thirty-four years old. I've spent my life developing my military career. I've focused on nothing else." A little sigh escaped him. "But now all that's over. I'm starting a new career. In a new town. I'm starting a new life. With Timmy."

She wasn't certain where he was going with this. Didn't know quite where her help fit in.

"You see," he said again, "I'm single. I've spent a

tiny fraction of time around children. None really, except the months Timmy stayed with me..." He trailed off. "What do I say to him? What do I do? How do I act? How do I react? What if...?"

Anna knew he was asking questions, but his words sounded kind of hazy. She'd stopped focusing on his conversation when he'd said the word *single*. Oh, her intuition had told her that he wasn't married. Timmy's file had done so also. But, for the life of her, she couldn't figure out why she felt so elated when he'd professed his marital status.

The fact that she'd responded so strongly to his pronouncement should have triggered warning bells inside her head. But it hadn't.

He was looking at her expectantly, and she felt acutely embarrassed that she'd let her attention wander.

"Look, you can help me," he said, his tone a little more potent now, even tinged with desperation. "You talk to kids all day long. You work with them week in and week out." He slid to the edge of his seat. "How about giving me some parenting lessons?"

She inhaled so quickly that she nearly choked. "B-but Mr. Cheney, I'm no parent." As she said the words, her heart fluttered in her chest painfully. This man would never know how it hurt her to reveal that fact. "I don't see how I can—"

"Of course you can," he interrupted. "All I'm asking is that you spend a little time with Timmy and me. Give me some pointers on how...on how to be with a kid. Let me watch you with him. And you watch me. You can help me, Miss Maxwell. You can."

There was something about him—something about knowing what he'd given up for this child, something about the commitment he felt for Timmy, something about the urgency in his voice—that made her want to help him.

So it was without thinking about how the school principal would view her actions, it was without thinking about how the school counselor would feel about her toes being stepped on, and it was without thinking about how unprofessional her conduct might look to her fellow teachers, that she gave the man across from her a small smile.

"Okay," she said softly. "I'd be happy to spend some time with you and Timmy, Mr. Cheney."

The smile that lit his face nearly took her breath away. It seemed as though a load of worry had been lifted from the man's shoulders, and Anna thrilled to know she was the one who had lifted it.

"Derrick," he said, standing and offering her his hand. "Call me Derrick."

"And I'm Anna."

She slipped her hand into his. The warmth of his touch sent a myriad of sensations tingling across her skin. His grasp was firm and secure, and it should have activated that well-used, self-protecting alarm deep within her subconscious. But it simply hadn't.

Then again, maybe it had, and she had chosen to ignore it.

Chapter Two

"So, how'd things go with Timmy's teacher?"

Derrick sat in the dimly lit lounge of the Bowl-o-rama and looked across the table at his friend, Jason Devlin. "Okay," he said.

Jason was a police officer for the town of Bayview, and Derrick had gone to college with the man. He appreciated his friendship and felt the urge to go into greater detail than he normally would, but the sound of a heavy bowling ball smashing into wooden pins interrupted all conversation in the small room as a patron opened the glass door and exited the lounge.

"In fact," Derrick said, once the door had swung shut and the noise of the bowling alley was muted enough for him to be heard, "the meeting went better than okay. It went well."

"Oh?"

Derrick's other friend, Reece Newton, raised his brows as he made the query, absently swiping the frothy beer foam from his upper lip.

Reece, too, was a good friend and old college buddy. In fact, it was because of these two men that Derrick had decided to settle in Bayview with Timmy.

When Derrick had contacted his friends and told them about his dilemma concerning Timmy and his decision to quit the Navy, both Jason and Reece had suggested Bayview as a place to set up home and business. Both of the men had been quick to share the fact that they too were single fathers, raising their children alone. So the three of them had formed "The Club," a small threesome of single dads who looked to each other for support and encouragement in parental matters.

"Yeah, the meeting went very well," Derrick said, and then he went about explaining the details of his conversation with Miss Anna Maxwell.

When he'd summed up everything, Reece commented warily, "She offered to help you?"

"Well," Derrick said, "she *agreed* to help." He decided against telling his friends that he felt he'd coerced the woman. "She's going to spend some time with Tim and me," he went on. "Since she's with kids so much, I thought she could give me some pointers on dealing with him…you know, talking to him, trying to get to know him."

Reece scowled over the rim of his mug. "So, what you're saying is that the pointers I gave you aren't worth a tinker's damn."

"Hey, man," Derrick said, "I'm not saying that at all. I tried the suggestions you gave me. Every single one of them." He shook his head. "It's just that Timmy isn't athletically inclined the way your Jeffrey is. I know they're nearly the same age and all, but Tim just wasn't interested in the baseball mitt I bought him. Or the basketball. Or the football. Or the—"

"Okay, okay," Reece stopped him. "I get your drift."

"Timmy's just not into sports," Jason said to no one in particular. "He's more into reading...and science. Academic stuff."

"Yeah," Derrick said, helpless against the tiny frown that knit his brow, "and how do you deal with a kid like that?"

The rhetorical question hung in the air as all three of them sipped contemplatively on their frosty mugs of draft.

When next Derrick spoke, his voice was soft, as though he might be speaking to himself, and he said, "And if Timmy is into 'academic stuff,' why is he acting like a little hooligan in school?"

"To get the teacher's attention?" Jason suggested. "Man, I'm glad my little princess is only a baby." He grinned at Derrick. "It's not that I don't want to share your pain, friend. But I'm happy to wait a few years to do it."

"Thanks," Derrick grumbled good-naturedly.

Reece rested his elbows on the table as he leaned toward the other two men. "So, what's in it for this teacher? This Miss...uh...Miss—"

"Maxwell," Derrick said. "Anna Maxwell."

He let her name roll around on his tongue. The feel of it was colorful and lively, hot and silky, all at the same time. He found it startling. And pleasant.

"So, what's in it for Miss Anna Maxwell?" Reece repeated his question.

"Darn it, Reece!" Jason said.

Derrick nearly smiled at Jason's mild expletive. He

knew the man had been trying to curb his language since the birth of Gina Marie.

"You don't even know the woman," Jason continued heatedly. "Don't go putting her down and making assumptions before she's even had a chance to offer Derrick some solutions to Timmy's problems."

Reece's eyes narrowed in a silent scowl.

"Just because you chose a bad apple," Jason said, "doesn't mean the whole barrel is rotten."

As nonchalantly as possible, Derrick reached into the wicker basket that sat on the table and plucked out a pretzel, all the while feeling a frantic need to change the topic of conversation. Reece was surly enough this evening without getting into his memories of the "marriage from hell," as he called it.

"I thought I'd take her sailing," Derrick spouted off the top of his head. "That is, if neither of you plans to use the boat Saturday."

Derrick felt a surge of relief when both his friends indicated that he could have use of the sailboat that the three of them had purchased together this past summer. He'd been worried about having Anna over to the house—worried about what she'd think about all the silence. It just wasn't natural with a little boy about. And Derrick still failed to figure out how Timmy could be so quiet and obedient at home and so disruptive at school. It didn't make sense, and the situation made him feel so…out of control.

But Derrick would feel more confident and self-assured if the three of them were out on the water with the sea air blowing all around them.

Yes, he wanted Anna Maxwell's help, but he was determined that she not view him as inept or incapable of raising Timmy. Derrick knew he was up to the job.

His own father had done it alone, hadn't he? His own father had raised not only him, but Timmy's dad, James, as well. And he'd done it all by himself.

And look at the two men sitting across from you, he silently told himself. They, too, were raising their children alone.

So, Derrick knew it could be done. But for weeks now, he'd been fighting a huge, ugly dragon that he called doubt. If he were to tell Reece and Jason about this battle raging inside him, he was certain they would laugh him into oblivion.

He simply had to keep telling himself he could do it, that was all. If he said the words long enough, maybe he'd come to believe them.

But that didn't seem to stop the terrible dragon from spitting fiery questions of uncertainty at him.

The bowling alley manager waved to them from across the lounge. "Your lane is ready."

"Thanks," Derrick called out to the man.

As the three of them rose from the table and made their way to the door, Jason said, "Hey guys, Gina's diaper rash is much better."

Reece pulled open the door of the lounge that led to the bowling alley. "Great," he said. "I know she's been uncomfortable."

"Yeah," Jason said. "The pediatrician gave me some ointment. And Gina's bottom is getting less red everyday."

Derrick stifled a grin. It was great to focus on someone *else's* problem with child rearing—even if the problem *was* diaper rash.

Anna approached the one-level, ranch-style house and pressed her hand to her abdomen. It seemed that the curiosity she was feeling over seeing Derrick interact with Timmy had her stomach fluttering like dozens of butterfly wings. At least she *thought* the reason for her anxiety was seeing Derrick interact with Timmy—no, she was certain it was. She inhaled deeply of the sea air in an attempt to calm her nerves.

As she used the shiny brass door knocker to announce her presence, she couldn't help but admire the six-panel solid wood door. It had a deep luster finish that was set off by the raw cedar siding. This house was perfect for the natural setting of the bay.

Timmy opened the door. He didn't look surprised to see her, which meant that Derrick had told him she was coming and for that she was happy. Yet she couldn't read in his expression how he felt about her presence.

"Gee, Miss Maxwell," he said abruptly, "you're wearin' jeans."

She fought to suppress the grin that wanted to curl her lips, but she lost the war.

"Yes," she said. "Outside of school, I'm a normal person, just like you."

Evidently Timmy sensed she was teasing him, and he gave her a small smile.

She followed him toward the back of the house, thinking what a lonely child Timmy seemed. He didn't get along with the other children. He kept to himself, playing solitary games during recess or simply reading books.

From what Derrick had told her, Timmy hadn't spent much time with kids his own age. Maybe, she thought, he simply didn't know how to relate. Maybe he didn't know how to deal with relationships with his peers. Socialization was a learned skill, everyone who worked with children knew that fact. Maybe Timmy just hadn't been taught the art of making friends.

It wasn't the first time these thoughts had passed through her mind since her meeting with Derrick. She vowed yet again to observe Timmy carefully—with his godfather and with his classmates.

Timmy pulled open the sliding glass door, and the two of them stepped out onto the deck.

The view of Pocomoke Sound was utterly breathtaking, and she could see two—no, three—small islands out in the distance in the Chesapeake Bay. The gray-blue water was dotted with boats as people took advantage of this beautiful, sunny October day.

"Hello, there!"

She whirled around at the sound of Derrick's voice.

"Hi," she said.

Anna had meant to say more, but the sight of him was as breathtaking as the view of the bay had been only a moment before. He was dressed casually, in khaki-colored, cotton shorts, a white knit pullover and dock shoes. His bare legs were tanned and muscular. As he picked up the life jackets, his biceps knotted into tight mounds, the muscle running from his elbow to wrist was corded and well defined. There wasn't an ounce of fat on the man.

She remembered he'd told her he was starting his own accounting firm in Bayview, but he certainly didn't fit her image of someone who made his living sitting behind a desk. Derrick Cheney was a dyed-in-the-wool outdoorsman. He looked like he belonged on the water, not in some stuffy office.

"You're early," he told her.

She swallowed, a little taken aback at his abruptness. "Sorry," she said.

Then he smiled, his handsome countenance lightening tremendously.

"Luckily, I'm ahead of schedule." He added a third jacket to his load. "Let me take these down to the dinghy and we'll push off."

She watched him walk down the grassy slope toward the water.

"Miss Maxwell," Timmy said quietly, "am I in trouble?"

"In trouble?" She turned her full attention to the boy.

"Yeah." He looked out at the water's edge. "How come you're here? Uncle Derrick said you were coming—" his gaze returned to her face "—but he didn't say why. So...am I in some kind of trouble?"

"Oh, honey," she said, "you're not in trouble." But then she hesitated. She didn't know how to tell him why she was here. She had no idea what Derrick wanted Timmy to know. What he didn't want the child to know. Suddenly she felt on very shaky ground.

"Really," she said weakly, "you're not in trouble."

Timmy was an intelligent child, Anna knew from experience. He obviously realized she hadn't fully answered his questions as to her presence here. But before he could inquire further, she asked, "Is there any way we can help? Anything we can carry down to the water?"

"Uncle Derrick packed up a picnic lunch. I'll go get it."

"No, no." Derrick said the words in a rush as he trotted the final few steps back to the deck.

Timmy had made the offer with a surprising and sudden burst of gusto. But she watched the eagerness in Timmy's face dissolve to meek obedience, and the child took a step backward.

"I'll get the cooler," Derrick said to Timmy. "You and Anna...er...a...Miss Maxwell...can go down to the dinghy."

"Yes, sir," Timmy mumbled.

Derrick disappeared into the house, and she stepped off the deck onto the grass. The slope down to the water's edge was gradual, and it offered a fantastic view. Yet she barely noticed the picturesque scene as she pondered what had just taken place between Derrick and Timmy.

Why had Derrick stifled the child's attempt to help? she wondered. And the submissive way in which Timmy had surrendered made her realize that this wasn't the first time he'd felt thwarted. She made a mental note to discuss this with Derrick.

When the two of them arrived at the small dinghy, she reached toward the life jackets.

"Do you think we should go ahead and slip into these?" she asked.

Timmy didn't answer her right away, and when she glanced at him, he was staring up at the house, a look of confusion and indecision on his young face.

"Well," he said slowly, "maybe we should wait."

She, too, looked toward the house and saw Derrick coming out of the sliding glass doors. He was encumbered with a large cooler and not one, but two brown paper bags. He set his load down on the deck and locked the door behind him before picking everything up and making his way toward them.

The silly man, Anna thought. Why hadn't he allowed Timmy to lug some of that stuff? And for that matter, why hadn't he asked her to help, also? He certainly looked as though he could use it!

She dropped the life jacket at her feet and hurried to him.

"Here," she said. "Let me have some of that."

"I'm fine," he told her.

"Yeah," she muttered. "And you're going to break your back while I watch."

She took the two bags from the top of the cooler.

"I said I was okay."

The tone of his voice made it evident to her that her actions utterly confused him.

Derrick loaded the supplies into the rowboat.

"Okay, everybody into a jacket," he instructed.

He bent and picked up a life jacket. And like a little lemming, Timmy followed suit. As she watched the interaction between Derrick and his godson, Anna slid her arms into an orange jacket and snapped the strap securely.

Even though their day together was just starting, this outing was turning into a very eye-opening experience. She was making some remarkable discoveries concerning Timmy. And Derrick. She couldn't wait to discuss her thoughts with the man.

Without being told, she climbed into the boat and sat down. Derrick was next to step in. He turned to Timmy.

"You coming?" he asked his godson.

The child's chin tipped up. "Sure I am," he said.

But he said the words too boldly, too loudly, and Anna shifted in her seat to look at his face.

There was fear in his eyes. Not a lot. But it was there just the same.

"Timmy, if you don't want to go," she quickly offered, "we can find something to do right here."

"Nonsense," Derrick said. "Didn't you just hear him say he was coming?"

His question was boisterous, almost forced, and it made Anna realize just how hard he was trying to make things go perfectly. Derrick offered Timmy his hand, and the boy wavered only a split second before he took it.

Timmy settled on the seat beside her and Derrick took up the oars. The short trip to the moored sailboat could have been jerky and uncomfortable, but Anna knew it was Derrick's expert handling of the small craft that made the ride smooth.

Derrick was the first to board the bigger boat. He tied off the dinghy securely and then gave both Anna and Timmy a hand into the sailboat.

"It's gorgeous!" Anna smoothed her hand along the wooden rail, its deep, glossy finish glinting in the bright light of the clear morning. The brass fittings were buffed and shined, reflecting the sun's rays like so many mirrors.

As he unloaded the supplies from the dinghy, he said, "Thanks. I went in with a couple of my buddies and we bought it this past spring when Tim and I first moved to Bayview." He stopped long enough to look up at the single, tall mast. "She's small, but she sails smoothly."

He went down the short flight of steps into the cabin where she heard him putting away the food and other things he'd brought aboard with him. She looked over at Timmy who sat quietly, but the whiteness of his knuckles as he clutched the edge of the bench seat made it obvious to her that all was not right with the boy.

Anna moved to sit next to him. "Timmy," she said very softly, "are you afraid of going out into the bay?"

His brow furrowed and he gave a disgusted sound. "No way."

But there was fear in his eyes. She read it as easily as if it were a page in a book. However, before she could question him further, Derrick reappeared.

"Let's get underway." He cranked a winch that raised the large sail high into the air.

Anna glanced at Timmy and saw him eyeing the loose end of the rigging as though he wanted to tie off the line. But he didn't make a move toward it. Derrick grabbed the rope and fastened it in a figure eight on a brass cleat. He did the same to a small sail in the front—or bow—of the boat.

As Derrick made his way back toward them and the tiller, the boat gently drifted with the wind at its side. He disconnected the braided line from the mooring and then positioned the boom.

"Let's make way," he called.

Almost as though he'd called the wind itself, the sails filled and began to pull. Anna was struck by the sheer joy expressed in Derrick's face. The wind blew his sandy-blond hair back from his forehead, and the smile on his lips was euphoric. He was most definitely born to be a seafaring man.

But even as she looked at the tall, handsome man steering the boat, her brain worried over little Timmy. The child was so obviously afraid—either of the sailboat or of the water, she didn't know which. Yet he'd refused to speak up when she'd asked him about it. Also, Timmy had wanted to help, both on shore and here on the boat, but he hadn't been able to for one reason or another. On shore Derrick had kept him from helping to carry some of the supplies. And then as his godfather had been raising the sails, Timmy had wanted to pitch in, Anna could see it, but he hadn't. All these things made her wonder what was happening between this boy and this man.

Derrick entertained them with stories of his exploits and experiences in the Navy. And in between the tales—half of which Anna suspected were as tall as the mast on the boat—he steered the boat, tacking first in one direction and then another, as they zigzagged along the bay.

She would have liked to have gotten lost in the stories he told. His face became so animated, his chocolaty eyes glinting in the sunlight. He nearly mesmerized her. But thoughts of Timmy kept nagging at the back of her brain, and she glanced at him often.

The child tried to enjoy himself, that was evident in the smile that pressed his lips back forcefully. But his shoulders were tense, and he never relinquished his tight hold on the bench seat.

Couldn't Derrick see that Timmy was miserable?

She reached over and covered the boy's hand with hers in what she hoped would be a comforting gesture, but he slid over a scant inch and pulled himself free of her touch. Anna realized it was a clear sign that he didn't want her *or* his godfather to notice how he was feeling.

"Okay," Derrick said suddenly. "Let's push her till her ribs spread."

He came about and let the wind catch the sails. Anna looked anxiously at Timmy and saw that his grip on the bench was now tighter than before. Her chest filled with compassion and she wanted badly to tell Derrick to take them ashore. But she didn't want Timmy to feel embarrassed in front of his godfather or become angry at what he might see as her interference. So she didn't say anything. She simply sat there feeling wretched.

Finally it was obvious that Timmy could take it no more, for he said, "Excuse me, sir. May I go below?"

Derrick's smile never faded. "Sure, Timmy. Go ahead."

The man must be blind as a bat, Anna thought. How could he not see Timmy's anguish? How could he not notice the child's fear?

She watched Derrick watch Timmy disappear into the cabin and she continued to marvel at his stupidity where children were concerned.

He raised his gaze to hers. "Things are going great today, huh?"

Her eyes narrowed to a glare. "You really think so?"

Chapter Three

Derrick's face became a mask of total bewilderment. "What?" he asked. "What are you saying?"

Her glare narrowed even further. "I refuse to discuss it when there's a chance Timmy will hear," she whispered, darting a quick glance toward the small doorway that led to the cabin and then back at Derrick.

A deep crease wrinkled Derrick's forehead, and his brown eyes held a multitude of questions, but he remained silent for the longest time. Finally he said, "We can talk soon. Timmy goes below and falls asleep every time we come out on the bay." The barest hint of a smile played across his mouth. "The sea air does that to him."

Evidently he'd expected his words to reassure her, but what he said only served to stir her anger further. He looked taken aback when her lips thinned with the fury she felt. She watched his jaw muscle tense and relax, tense and relax, in obvious frustration.

Well, he'd simply have to feel frustrated, she decided fiercely. How any man could have all the answers staring him right in the face and not see them was beyond her.

"'The sea air does that to him.'" Her disgruntled mutter became lost on the bay breeze. Did Derrick really believe that? The reason Timmy retreated below deck was so plainly obvious to her, she had to wonder why Derrick didn't see it for himself.

Was the man that naive where children were concerned?

And to think that, whatever fear Timmy was experiencing, he'd experienced it before; he'd felt the need to escape to the cabin, escape to the safe haven of sleep every time he went out sailing.

Minutes passed. The beauty of this gorgeous day was marred by her deep concern for Timmy. She was aware of the salt-tinged wind blowing, the sun shining, the water slapping against the hull of the boat, but she simply wasn't able to enjoy all those things. Not after what she'd learned about Timmy.

That poor child.

She ran agitated fingers through her long hair and sighed. If she was going to talk to Derrick, she needed to get her emotions under control. If she didn't, she just might lose her temper and end up shouting at the man. He obviously didn't know what was happening with Timmy—even if it *was* happening right under his nose.

Closing her eyes and lifting her face to the sunshine, Anna tried to think peaceful thoughts. She was certain that Derrick was oblivious to what Timmy was feeling: the boy's frustration at wanting to help and not being allowed to; his fear, of what she was still uncertain, but she suspected it was either the boat or the water. Yes, Derrick was unaware of these things.

He had gone through so much—literally changed his life for the child. If he'd had any inkling of what Timmy felt he'd surely have...

Movement at the stern of the boat drew her attention. She turned her head and silently watched as Derrick tied off the tiller and disappeared below deck. When he came back up, he closed the hatch behind him and his curt nod told her that Timmy was asleep.

Derrick handed her a bottle of chilled fruit juice. "I want to talk," he told her. "Just give me a minute to get things under control."

He went forward and released the line that held the mainsail taut. Quickly and efficiently, he lowered the sail and folded the heavy material accordion fashion over the boom. Anna saw how tense and serious his handsome face had become. Her anger was gone now, it had dissipated in the wake of the realization that Derrick honestly didn't understand what Timmy was feeling. She inhaled deeply, wrestling with a sudden indecision over exactly how she should go about telling him all the things she'd discerned during the past couple of hours.

All she knew was that she had to tell him. She had to be up front and honest with the man. It's what he'd asked her to do, wasn't it?

But after years of working with the parents of her students, she'd learned that adults rarely wanted exactly what they asked for. Time and again mothers and fathers had come to her for honest opinions concerning their children. And Anna had found it prudent to temper the truth with a little compassion.

It wasn't her intent to hurt Derrick's feelings. However, it was imperative that he change his "parental tactics" where his godson was concerned.

But how do you tell someone that he's going about raising a child all wrong? How do you tell him that his idea of a father's role is slightly off kilter?

One word whispered softly through her mind... *gently.*

Derrick dropped anchor and the sailboat swayed in the slow current of the bay. Then he came close to her, easing himself down onto the bench seat beside her.

"Okay—"

He spoke the single word and then she watched his throat muscles convulse in a tight swallow—an action that caused her insides to curl with some unexpected, unnameable heat.

"—tell me."

When she didn't speak right away, he reached out, pulled the bottle of juice from her hand and twisted off its lid. He handed the bottle back to her.

She grasped the juice, feeling the cool condensation on the smooth exterior of the glass moisten her fingertips. Anna fought the urge to press the chilled bottle to her suddenly warm cheek.

Why should she feel this hesitation? she wondered. He wanted her opinion—he'd asked for it.

Anna looked at the tight lines of strain around his eyes, strain she wanted desperately to ease by making him smile. *This is silly,* she thought. These unwitting emotions she was feeling—the undefinable warmth in her gut, the desire to ease his stress—might lead someone who didn't know the situation between herself and Derrick to think that the man meant more to her than he should.

This is silly, she repeated silently to herself and

shoved the idea aside. But the thought of relieving his stress remained in her mind just long enough for her to decide it would be best to ease into delivering her bad news.

"I *have* seen some things between you and Timmy that I think we should discuss," she told him softly. "But first I want to ask you a question."

"Okay." His brow knitted together. "Go ahead."

She focused every ounce of her attention on Derrick and inhaled deeply, only vaguely aware now of the fresh sea air around her.

Cocking her head a fraction to one side, she said, "When you went below just now, you tied off the tiller. Why didn't you ask me to take over for you for the few minutes that you were gone?"

The breeze blew a strand of her hair across her face, and she reached up instinctively to smooth it back.

"And when you lowered the sail," she said, before he could respond, "I could tell it wasn't an easy job for one. Why didn't you ask for my help?" The air felt suddenly heavy and she chuckled lightly in an effort to alleviate the tension that was gathering around them like thick clouds. "I mean, I know I'm not as experienced as you are on the water, but I certainly could have helped—"

She stopped abruptly when she saw the apologetic expression on his face.

"Oh, Derrick." Anna reached out and placed a reassuring hand on his sun-warmed thigh. "Please don't get the wrong idea. I'm not insulted."

Anna would have believed it impossible for his frown to deepen. She was wrong.

"I don't understand," he said, his tone grating with the confusion he was obviously feeling.

She licked her lips and slid a little straighter on the seat. "I'm trying to prove a point. And I'm trying to prove it without attacking your relationship with Timmy."

Derrick shook his head. "Now I'm really at a loss," he told her. "I didn't ask for your help lowering the mainsail, but what does that have to do with my relationship with Timmy?"

"Just bear with me for a moment." As she made her plea, she lightly pressed her fingertips into the rock-hard muscle just above his knee.

The feel of his firm leg beneath her touch made her eyes dart to her hand. She hadn't realized she'd continued to touch him. That spiraling heat returned with a vengeance deep in her belly, and she became startlingly aware of how the soft, springy hair on his leg tickled her palm, how solid his thigh felt under her fingers, how hot his skin—

She pulled her hand back and rested it on her lap, hoping she didn't look as self-conscious as she felt. Her cheeks flushed hot, and she glanced out at the thin strip of land across the bay.

The sound of her heart pounded in her ears, and she made a frantic scramble to get hold of herself. She cleared her throat and directed her gaze at Derrick.

"You've spent a lot of years alone," she began, relieved that her voice sounded quite normal. "You're a strong man. You've become self-sufficient. Dependent on no one but yourself."

"I'd agree with that."

Anna could tell by his tone that he had no idea where the conversation was going. But despite his uncertainty, he was showing a huge amount of patience, and that helped her to relax.

"That's not a bad thing, in and of itself," she said. "But it could cause…problems. It could…" She let the sentence trail and felt the hefty weight of frustration press on her as she searched for words that would explain her thoughts yet at the same time wouldn't offend his masculinity.

Derrick leaned over and took her hand. "Look, Anna," he said. "I have no idea what you're getting at. I'm sorry I didn't ask for your help with the boat. Yes, I've spent most of my life on my own. Yes, I stand on my own two feet. I'm sure in my ability to take care of myself." He shook his head the tiniest bit. "But for the life of me, I can't figure out how all this fits in with Timmy." He grinned at her. "The point you're trying to make seems pretty disjointed to me."

Before she was able to take offense, he slid his other hand over top of hers. His skin was warm and smooth.

"Now, I know I've made some kind of huge blunder where Tim is concerned," he went on. "And whatever I did, it caused you to look at me a few minutes ago as though I were some kind of monster. So I want you to stop beating around the bush and spit it out. I can take it." The smile he gave her was boyishly charming. "I mean, you've already told me I've got a strong character."

Anna couldn't help but return his smile. "So I did," she said.

Then Derrick shrugged. "I got the impression, though, that that's somehow part of the problem."

His golden brown eyes glinted with sunlight.

"You're going to have to help me understand that," he said. "I always thought that having a strong character was a good trait. I thought that being independent and self-reliant were good things."

Very good things, Anna said silently.

Finally she found her voice. "But things are a little different when it comes to family." She stared up at him, hoping she'd get the words right. "That's what you and Timmy have become, you know."

"But I should no longer be strong and independent?"

"I'm suggesting," she began slowly, "that you try being less strong, less independent. You need to be strong enough that Timmy knows he can depend on you." Here she faltered slightly, but forced herself to go on. "But you need to depend on Timmy, too."

Derrick was frowning again. "But he's a six year old child."

"That doesn't matter." Anna set down the now warm juice and brushed her fingers through her hair. "Timmy needs to feel needed. Otherwise he won't feel part of the family unit."

Anna tried hard to ignore the humming that radiated along her skin. The electric vibrations began when Derrick had sandwiched her hand between his. The urge to protect herself, to withdraw from him was great, but she fought it for the simple reason that her intuition told her he needed the physical support of touching her. Whether his need came from a conscious or subconscious level, she couldn't tell.

"Let me get this straight," Derrick said. "I need to need Tim. But how—"

"Not necessarily," she interrupted. "We both know that you can survive without your godson. We both know that the need is pretty one-sided here. Timmy needs you to provide for him—a place to live, food to eat, clothes to wear. He needs you for emotional support. He needs you to love him." She looked into his face. "But it's going to be imperative that you allow him to feel needed, too."

There it was, that frown again. Anna barely squelched the urge to reach up and smooth the pad of her thumb across his forehead. He was being more open-minded, more tolerant of her opinion than she ever thought this headstrong man would be.

"I think I may be getting it," he said at last. "I have to make Tim believe that I need him."

Her heart swelled with warmth and it showed in her wide smile. "That's exactly right," she said. "And the great thing about it is that it should be pretty easy to do."

The chuckle that escaped from his throat was full of relief. "So, you *are* going to give me some suggestions. You don't know how glad I am of that."

His laugh was a rich, pleasing sound that started her heart pattering in her chest. He was so very handsome, especially when his features were softened with a smile. Anna found her mind drifting—something that wasn't a rare occurrence for her.

"Suggestions," she reminded herself aloud. "Yes, well…what you need to do is give Timmy some responsibilities. Does he have chores to do around the house? Your home is his home now, and he should be responsible for its upkeep."

"But, Anna," he lightly scoffed, "the child's only six."

"Don't let that get in the way," she said. "Make him keep his room clean. Take out the garbage. Dry the dishes. Anything. He may not do the jobs as well as you could do them, but believe me, making him responsible for some small chores will be the easiest way for you to make him feel like you need him."

"What makes you think he'll want to help out around the house?" he asked.

Remembering the indecision on Timmy's face and his suppressed urge to help gather the supplies for this sailing trip, Anna said, "Oh, I think he'll be eager to lend a hand."

"You really think so?"

Anna grinned. "Very eager."

"Okay," he said, shrugging one shoulder a fraction. "I'll give it a try. It does make sense. In the Navy each member of the crew had a job to do." He gazed out at the water, his tone lowering as though he was talking to himself. "A job that made him a responsible member of his division."

"Well, now," Anna commented, "I don't know that you'll be able to run your home like the Navy runs a ship. Kids are too unpredictable for that."

His dark eyes were once more on her.

Even though they were out on the wide expanse of the bay, a light breeze blowing about them, the serious expression that sobered his handsome face seemed to take every molecule of oxygen out of the air. Anna felt herself freeze, as though she was waiting for something dramatic to happen.

Time seemed to slow, and she felt mesmerized by the mysterious aura that suddenly seemed to enfold them.

Although she hadn't actually seen Derrick move, she was aware that he'd slid closer to her. One of his arms rested along the side of the boat behind her back, the other still grasped her hand. They were pressed together side by side, thigh to thigh, hip to hip.

"You're one intelligent lady, Anna Maxwell," he

said, his voice caressing her like some richly scented fragrance.

Her first instinct was to negate his compliment, but his tone was thick with sensuality—sensuality that overwhelmed her to the point that she wasn't able to put two coherent words together.

A tiny voice in the back of her mind told her that this wasn't right, that there was a reason she shouldn't allow herself to be swept away by this gorgeous man. The same tiny voice reminded her that there was something else she'd intended on telling Derrick. Something important. Something that had to do with Timmy. But for the life of her, she couldn't bring the information to the forefront of her brain. Not when such utter confusion was reigning there at the moment.

"I'm so glad you agreed to help me with Timmy."

His words were heady. And the sound of his sincere gratitude only acted to further intoxicate her already stuporous thoughts. The tiny voice of warning and reason was completely obliterated as something new and exciting overtook her mind.

Desire.

She wanted to be near this man. Closer than she was now. She wanted to tug off his shirt and flatten her palms against his broad chest. Wanted to feel his arms tighten around her. Wanted to press her nose to the curve of his neck and smell the heated scent of his skin. Wanted to taste the salt from the air that surely clung to his lips.

Her brain was fogged with the wanting she felt. Her gaze was riveted to his, and she could tell that he knew exactly what it was she was feeling. And she didn't care.

She didn't care because she could clearly read in the

golden brown velvet of his eyes that he was feeling the same hunger as she.

He bent his head, and she felt his breath caress the tender flesh at the back of her neck.

"Thank you, Anna."

A heated shiver coursed across her skin, and her mouth curled into a languid smile.

His lips brushed the outer edge of her ear, and she heard the rhythmic sound of his breathing—a sound that set her heart to racing in her chest.

The wild, frantic emotions that charged through her entire body were so at odds with the tortoiselike pace that life had seemed to take on in the small world of this sailboat.

Even though she was expecting it, wanting it, dying for it, his first kiss came as a complete surprise. The pressure of his lips directly behind her ear had her half-closed eyes opening wide and her breath leaving her in a tiny gasp.

Immediately she closed her eyes and tilted her head, giving him full range of her neck. He didn't disappoint her.

She inhaled slowly, deeply when she felt him take the lobe of her ear between his teeth. Then he pressed his nose into her hair and breathed in its scent, and she found the action highly erotic. He planted his mouth on the back curve of her jaw, the feel of him tasting her skin caused a heat to flush over her entire body— a heat she knew had nothing whatsoever to do with the full, midday October sun that blazed overhead.

His thumb had been leisurely playing over the hills and valleys of her knuckles, but now he raised his hand, catching her chin in his fingers. Ever so slowly, he turned her face toward his.

The intensity of his gaze was like a physical touch, and when she opened her eyes, she wasn't surprised to find him studying her features.

She wanted desperately to smile at him, to give him some sign of what she was feeling. But the magnitude of desire raging through her veins seemed to anesthetize her facial muscles, and all she could do was return his stare. However, she wasn't too concerned by the fact that she couldn't give him a smile, because she knew without a doubt that every emotion she was experiencing was displayed in her eyes. She felt sure of it.

He slid his fingers back along one side of her jaw, his thumb back along the other. When he tilted up her chin, her breath caught in her throat, and she was certain he meant to kiss her.

He loomed over her, his mouth a scant inch from hers. He was so close his shadow blocked the sun and she could feel his silky breath on her cheek.

It wasn't until he closed the distance by half that she felt the first jolt of warning from her brain. The tiny voice that had tried so hard before to be heard now screamed with a vengeance, warring with the hot and clamorous ringing and clanging of desire that held her a motionless captive.

In silence, with her mind fighting a mighty battle inside her head, Anna locked eyes with Derrick and watched him descend.

When his lips touched her, she lowered her eyelids and allowed her thoughts go completely blank. She wanted to enjoy this, savor every instant.

His mouth was firm and hot, silky and moist. His kiss was tentative, yet exploratory. His tongue cavorted lightly across her closed lips. He wasn't requesting entry just yet. It was obvious to Anna that he wanted to take this new experience slowly. And she was nearly able to smile in agreement.

Please, she heard herself say silently, *take your time.*

Suddenly his hand no longer cradled her chin. She felt a tug on her waist, and before she knew what was happening, he had scooped her up and settled her on his lap.

Now she found herself looking down into his face, and she found her own mouth hovering just above his.

Lord, how she wanted to weave her fingers behind his head. To be the aggressor and lower her mouth to his. But the little voice of warning in her brain screeched its little heart out, stamped its little foot. And she was forced to take notice.

But Derrick evidently had no idea what was happening inside Anna's head, and when she didn't act on the mutual desire that wrapped them in its tight embrace, he became a bit more assertive.

Delving his fingers in her hair, he pulled her to him. The kiss became instantly more energetic, filled with raw passion the likes of which she'd never before felt. All she wanted to think about was losing herself in this man's arms.

But that voice inside her refused to go away. It became frustrating and finally irritating.

"Afraid."

She whispered the word frantically against his lips. And when his eyes snapped open, she realized that she'd startled him just as much as she'd startled herself.

Where had the word come from? she wondered in hazy confusion.

He studied her intently for a few, heart-stopping moments. His jaw tensed as he swallowed and he pulled her close.

"Don't be," he said against her mouth. "Don't be." And his mouth was on hers once again.

His voice was rough with desire—so much desire that it almost overpowered the warning that thundered through her head. Almost, but not quite.

"No," she whispered between kisses. "No."

She pressed her flattened palm against his chest and tried to pull herself away from him. It was a feeble attempt at best and he held her to him with little more than a look.

The questions in his eyes matched the ones spinning around in her brain.

"It's not me who's afraid," she said, knowing she sounded as though she had more than one screw loose, but unable to help it, since she was working this out at the same time she was trying to explain it to him. "I'm not afraid."

She felt a sensuous chuckle vibrate deep in his chest. His mouth was cocked in a half grin that made her want to laugh with him, but the befuddled state she was in swept the thought away before it had even formed completely.

Stay focused, she silently berated herself.

"Well, *I'm* certainly not afraid," he whispered huskily. "This is a wonderful adventure we're having here. I refuse to let fear stand in the way."

The glint in his eyes was caused by more than simply the bright, autumnal afternoon sun. He wanted her. The message was crystal clear. And it made her feel joyous inside.

Smoothing her fingers along his jaw, she was nearly

sucked back into the whirling vortex of desire and need that threatened to drown all reason.

He was pulling her closer to him, ever closer. And just as his mouth was about to take her once again to paradise—

"Timmy!" The child's name burst from her lips, and she straightened her spine. And like a thunderstorm washes the dust from the air, saying the name had cleared her head of clutter so that she knew exactly what it was she'd meant to tell him about the boy and his fear.

The romantic atmosphere that had so thoroughly surrounded them just moments before dissolved in a flash. It was as if they'd been cuddling in a dark room and someone flipped on a bright overhead light.

It was awkward sitting there on his lap when the desire they had felt was completely and utterly gone without a trace. And Anna couldn't help but notice how, upon hearing his godson's name, Derrick had lost every nuance of passion that had been etched in his handsome features only seconds ago.

"What, Anna?" he said. "What about Timmy?"

"It's the other thing I meant to tell you...." She felt so foolish sitting in so intimate a spot, so she shifted her weight until she was once again on the bench seat beside him. "I wanted to tell you that Timmy's afraid."

"I thought we were finished talking about Tim," he said. He rubbed his fingers across the back of his neck. "I'm not real sure I like your timing, but I do want to hear what you have to say."

So she did. She told him of the fear she read in the child's eyes when they had slipped into their life jackets. She told him of the white-knuckled grip Timmy

had kept on the edge of the seat. She told him how she
felt his going to sleep was a defense mechanism to
avoid the fear he felt.

"Feeling afraid can exhaust a person," she said.

"Damn," Derrick whispered. "I can't believe I put
him through this. Time and time again, I forced him to
come out onto the bay. And I never saw the anxiety
he was feeling."

He moved to the other side of the boat and began to
pull up the anchor.

"Don't be too hard on yourself," Anna told him.
"Timmy doesn't want you to know."

He swiveled around to face her. "What?"

She told him about her attempt to comfort Timmy
by holding his hand and how the boy had scooted away
from her. "He's proud," she said. "I suspect he
doesn't want you look down on him for whatever it is
he's afraid of."

"But that's silly."

She shrugged. "Not to him."

Derrick moved to the stern and tugged on the line
that would start the outboard motor.

"You won't mind if we don't sail back, will you?"
he asked.

"Of course not."

"I want to get back to shore as soon as possible."

Derrick's face was full of determination and worry
as he turned the boat and headed for home. Anna
reached for the bottle of sun-warmed juice that sat
within close reach. She took a sip, but didn't even taste
it.

Just as Timmy's fear had exhausted him until he felt
the need to fall into a deep sleep, the myriad of riotous
emotions Anna had experienced had taken away every

bit of her strength. She didn't know what to think about what had happened between herself and Derrick. She didn't know what to feel. Her emotionally numbed brain told her it was best to think and feel nothing. At least for the time being.

So, taking another sip of the tasteless fruit juice, that's exactly what she did.

Chapter Four

Anna stared at the telephone, mentally debating the issue of whether or not to call.

The past four days had been fraught with emotional upheaval. She knew for a fact that she had a tendency to be...unfocused at times. But since going sailing with Derrick and Timmy last weekend, she'd been unable to keep her mind on any one thing for longer than a few seconds—unless that one thing was Derrick. Then she didn't seem to have even the smallest problem keeping her thoughts on track.

She was beginning to think she was obsessing on the man, and she knew very well that wasn't a healthy thing. But, Lord, when she thought about that kiss...

No, she silently ordered herself, *do not think about that.*

Snatching up the telephone receiver, she held it in her lap as she scanned Timmy's file to locate Derrick's number.

The information in the manila file folder blurred together, and the buzz from the telephone line sounded far off as thoughts of Saturday came swimming into her head.

She had been elated that Derrick had immediately returned the sailboat to shore when she'd relayed to him her idea of Timmy's fear. Derrick was so quick to do the right thing where his godson was concerned, often ignoring his own opinions and desires. Anna was certain now that his priorities were in the right place, and she had no doubt he'd do a wonderful job of raising Timmy. The road might be a little bumpy at times, but every adult bringing up a child, natural-born parent or not, experienced a few rough rides along the way.

He'd been very open to her suggestion that he not confront Timmy in her presence. She'd explained how she thought Timmy's pride might be damaged if he were made to confess his fear in front of his teacher. Derrick had readily agreed that this was a topic that needed to be discussed between just the two of them.

Helplessly, Anna found herself slipping into that dreamy state of reminiscence as her mind conjured unbidden images of the moments on the boat when she was alone with Derrick. Closing her eyes, she could once again feel his warm, silky breath caress the sensitive flesh at the curve of her neck. She easily remembered the sensual sensation of his lips pressing on the tender spot just behind her ear. The taste of sea salt on his skin. The heated male scent of him. The touch of his fingers entwining in her hair. The pounding of her heart. The rush of hot blood coursing through her veins. The sizzling desire that pulsed a rhythmic beat, steadily accelerating, deep in the very core of her being—

"Stop!" Anna's eyes flew open and she pressed her

free hand to her chest, marveling at how it rose and fell as she took in small, breathless gasps of air.

The memory was so clear, so vivid. It was almost as if she were once again nestled on Derrick's lap, once again feeling his arms about her, once again tasting his luscious kiss. Her ability to summon up her experience with him in such crystalline images had shocked her—and had made her life over the past four days absolutely miserable. But it wasn't only images that her mind could so easily conjure. Tastes and sounds were so easily recalled. She remembered the feel of his sun-heated skin on hers with a striking realism that threatened to actually suck her into the past.

Anna shook her head. This was like nothing she'd ever experienced before. Derrick Cheney had left a distinct and salient impression in her mind—an intense mark that was his alone.

She stared off across the room with unseeing eyes. No matter how much she wanted to blame this on Derrick, she knew deep in her heart that there was something else about her experience with the man that caused the memory of it to come back to her so readily and so often. And no matter how badly she wanted to deny it, no matter how desperately she wished to ignore what she was feeling, she knew that the name of that something was *desire*.

The raw, blinding passion she had felt for Derrick had swept her away to the point where there was nothing else. There was no small boy with problems hiding in sleep belowdeck, there was no Bayview, no Chesapeake Bay, no state of Maryland, no world around her. There was only one man and one woman, and the urgent desire to feel, to taste, to touch.

It was shocking to her to realize how she'd very

nearly lost her identity during the moments she'd allowed herself to become overwhelmed by Derrick's kiss.

She pressed her lips together in self-annoyance. *There you go again,* she told herself, *pointing the finger of blame at him when you are just as much at fault.*

At that moment she became aware that the droning dial tone of the telephone line had been replaced by the soft, recorded voice of an operator requesting her to "please hang up and try your call again."

Pressing the button that disconnected the line, Anna sighed. She wanted terribly to deny what she was feeling for Derrick. She'd love to be able to turn a blind eye to the desire she felt for him. But that would be silly and futile. It was better to know up front the monsters you needed to battle with. Realizing that her desire was a monster that must be slain did not surprise or shock her in the least. Several times in the past she had been in relationships, and she'd experienced the rejection and felt the hurt when she had to reveal her condition, disclose what she could and could not give.

The thought of being hurt and rejected by Derrick nearly made her frantic. She didn't stop to wonder why. All she knew was that she didn't dare allow a relationship between them to develop. It was imperative that she not see the repulsion and scorn in his brown eyes, not hear the contempt in his words that would be inevitable if they were to grow any closer to each other than they were right now.

However, that didn't change the fact that she was Timmy's teacher, that she'd promised to help Derrick cultivate the budding relationship between him and his godson. Before leaving him on Saturday, she'd promised to call him to let him know how Timmy was doing in school, and she *was* curious to discover how he'd made out when he'd confronted Timmy about his fears regarding the boat.

Anna pressed the numbers and tried to ignore the anxiety she felt building in the pit of her stomach as she listened to the ringing at the other end of the telephone line. Just because she recognized she had a monster to destroy didn't make the task any easier, it just made the idea more…real.

"Hello."

Recognizing his voice, Anna said, "Derrick? It's Anna." Before he could respond, she went on, "Have I called too late?"

"Oh, no," he said. "In fact, this is a perfect time to talk—"

Anna detected the pleasure in his tone at hearing from her and tried to disregard the delight that swelled in her chest like a powerful wave.

"—seeing as how I've just sent Tim upstairs for his bath." There was a moment of silence before he added, "I've missed you, Anna."

The joyous rush she had felt just a second before metamorphosed into a huge lump of panic that lodged in her throat. Suddenly it was hard to breathe, and her words were totally blocked off by the hard knot. Placing her free hand at the base of her neck, she drew in a slow, labored breath.

"Anna?" he called quizzically. "Are you there?"

"Yes." The tiny word came out as a whisper. She cleared her throat and tried again. "Yes, I'm here. I told you I'd call and let you know how things were going with Timmy at school." She hated the breathless quality of her voice and vowed to slow down her speech so she wouldn't sound so rushed, so out of control. "I implemented some ground rules for the children. Very elementary principles of good manners. Saying *thank you* and *please*, patiently waiting for a turn, acting with self-respect and respecting the rights of others, that kind of thing. It seems to be working out just fine. Timmy's learning the value of his friends, and all the children are benefiting from the lesson."

"I think it does make sense," Derrick said, "since Timmy's spent the majority of his years with adults, that he doesn't realize other children have rights, too, that his peers deserve the same sort of respect he'd give to you or me."

"Of course, it's only been a few days," she said. "But I really do believe this is the answer to his problem."

"Aren't you glad—"

Anna could hear the boyish grin in his voice, and even though she had no idea what he was about to say, she had to smile when she so easily pictured the charming expression on his handsome face.

"—I didn't allow you to send him to Special Ed?"

His words tempered her smile, but only a little.

"I'm happy to say that we've found what looks like a solution to Timmy's behavior problem," she told him. "But I still think that my idea of some counseling sessions wasn't a bad one."

"I'm just glad we were able to help Tim," he said. "Together."

Had he purposefully placed that sensual emphasis on the last word he spoke, or was it simply her imagination? She didn't dwell on the question, but rather asked one of her own.

"How are things there?"

"Oh, Anna, they couldn't be better. I told Tim that

I really needed his help around the house, and we sat down and came up with a list of chores for him to do.''

The sound of his chuckle made a silky shiver run up her spine.

''Of course,'' he continued, ''you were right when you told me he wouldn't be able to perform the jobs as well as I would, but I try hard to leave things alone and just live with the less-than-perfect results.''

Derrick sighed, and the sound of it so near to her ear made her feel he was close enough that she could reach out and touch him. If she were to simply close her eyes, she could conjure up an image of his handsome, perfect face with no trouble at all—

Dragging open her eyelids, Anna stifled a gasp. She had to stay focused!

''And we're actually spending time together,'' he went on. ''Quality time. He hardly ever closes himself in his room anymore.''

''That's good,'' she said. And then she felt her mouth tipping up in a smile, heard the warmth in her tone as she said, ''It's better than *good* actually. It's wonderful. I'm very happy for you and Timmy.''

Silent seconds ticked by, but the stillness was neither awkward nor uncomfortable.

''I talked to him,'' Derrick said, ''about his being afraid when we're out on the boat...''

He sighed, the sound of his exhalation a vivid reminder of his breath so close to her ear right before he'd kissed her. Just as on Saturday, the sound of it sent waves of electricity coursing across her skin.

''It took me a while to get the truth out of him,'' he said. ''But I finally was able to find out what was wrong. Can you believe he doesn't know how to swim?''

There was a sudden edge to his voice, and she knew she didn't need to respond to his question.

"I don't understand," he said, "how James could not have taken the time to see that his son had swimming lessons."

Anna wasn't surprised. Working with children year in and year out, she came into contact with many parents who just didn't have time for their children.

"So, I've offered to teach him myself. And he's accepted."

The quiet pride and obvious sense of success that flowed in the rich texture of his voice caused a chain reaction of emotions inside Anna. The first was pleasure. She was so happy to hear Derrick feeling self-assured about raising Timmy. She also felt gratified and content that she might have given him a little help in finding his way to this place of budding self-confidence. Then the feelings that arose inside her twisted just the tiniest bit, becoming more personal, more intimate. She cut them off as completely as she possibly could before they had time to actually form.

"I'm glad to hear that," she said, striving to remain as unemotional as possible. It was difficult, though, because she cared about Timmy. And Derrick.

Where the heck had that thought come from? She refused to allow herself to care about Derrick. She couldn't take the chance. Didn't think she would survive the inescapable hurt and pain he would cause her. Dear God, she couldn't let it happen.

"Oh," he said, "by the way..."

His rich chuckle reverberated in her ear and sent yet another shudder radiating along her spine. Darn it! Why did she allow this man to do this to her? As quickly as possible, she suppressed the shiver caused by the delicious sound of his gentle laugh and was so glad he wasn't actually here to see her reaction.

"Tim asked me an interesting question."

"Oh?"

"Yes," Derrick said. "He wanted to know why his teacher went sailing with us."

"And what did you tell him?"

She couldn't see his face, but she was certain she felt him smile.

"The truth," he said. "I told him that because I've spent so little time around kids his age, I needed some help. And what better place to find help—"

Again, a chuckle. Anna's grip tightened on the telephone receiver. Her palm grew moist and she discovered she'd unwittingly pressed her ear closer to the sound of his voice.

"—than from a teacher who spends her days working with six-year-olds?"

Forcing herself to relax, she asked, "And did he accept your explanation?"

"Oh, sure," he said. "But not before he clarified that some of the kids in his class were *seven*."

She smiled in spite of the chaotic state her emotions were in. "That doesn't surprise me," she told Derrick. "Timmy's a very intelligent, very *precise* child."

Anna felt a little better, seeing as how the conversation was focused solely on Timmy. She inhaled deeply, quietly, allowing some of the tension to leave her body as she slowly expelled the breath.

"When can I see you again?"

His quiet question took her completely off guard. She'd fully intended to keep Timmy the topic of conversation.

"Well...I...no...you see," she stammered. Nervous

adrenaline pumped through her body. Talking with Derrick made her feel as though she were on some turning, twisting amusement park ride—a ride that was deceptively calm one moment, whipping and thrashing the next.

Words, thoughts and partially formed phrases whirled through her mind like hailstones, pinging and pounding, until she felt the need to run and seek sanctuary.

This time the silence was more than awkward as she frantically sought for something to say.

"Anna?"

She couldn't bring herself to speak and, closing her eyes, she willed her heart to stop pounding in her chest.

"I'm here," she said, feeling as though she were about to come apart at the seams.

"Look," he told her, his voice like warm honey, "I'm very grateful for all that you've done for me and Timmy. Let me express my gratitude, let me take you to dinner."

She wanted to say yes. She wanted to see him again. But she knew it wasn't wise.

"That's not necessary," she told him, pleased at how she'd kept the words unemotional and stressed a professional tone.

"But—" he hesitated "—I'd really like to."

Anna heard the bewilderment that tinged his words. She hated to rebuff him, but it was easier to do it now than to wait until their relationship had progressed and *she* was the one left feeling abandoned and alone.

"I appreciate that," she told him. "But I just don't think it would be a good idea." Quickly, before he could respond and ask for reasons, she plowed on, "We've discovered a lot about Timmy recently. You two have begun to build a wonderful relationship. Keep working at it."

A wave of panic rolled over her, threatening to drown her calm facade. She felt a sudden desperation to end the conversation, end it now before he had a chance to bombard her with questions, before he had a chance to confront her with the desire they both knew they had felt for each other just four short days ago.

"I'll continue working with Timmy at this end," she said in a rush. "If you have any problems, feel free to call. But for right now, I think we have separate goals we need to strive toward."

She eased the receiver into its cradle on the base of the phone. The disconnection had been abrupt, she knew. She hadn't even said goodbye. But the brusque farewell had been unavoidable, for the emotion that swelled in her throat made it nearly impossible for her to speak another word.

Sadness wrapped itself around her. Unshed tears blurred her vision. She knew the sorrow she felt was for the loss of what might have been between herself and Derrick. But she had to protect herself. A relationship with him would never have worked out. Not when she was so very limited in what she could give him. As soon as he discovered that she was…defective, he'd leave her.

From the outer corner of her eye a tear trailed slowly down her cheek. She dashed it away.

"This is for the best," she proclaimed, her tone weak and shaky sounding. She inhaled deeply and cleared her throat, and in a stronger voice, she repeated, "For the best."

Anna took a covert glance across the classroom. Timmy wasn't himself today. She'd already heard him engage in a verbal battle this morning with Eric, one of his best friends in the class. Just as she was about to speak to the boys, little April, the resident peacemaker of the group, had intervened, and the incident had subsided. Anna liked it when her students worked out their differences for themselves.

Social skills were learned, and most all of her students had already had quite a bit of practice under their belts what with attending daycare and preschool. However, she knew from what Derrick had told her about Timmy that the child had had no exposure to other children his own age prior to coming into her first-grade classroom.

When she'd set down the rules two weeks ago, he'd seemed almost relieved to know there were boundaries. And he'd done so well following the regulations.

Lord, she couldn't believe it had only been two weeks since she'd last spoken with Derrick. The days had dragged by until she felt months had passed since her telephone call to him—the call during which she'd snuffed out any chance of a relationship with the man. He'd been interested. She knew that. But she couldn't allow—

No, she admonished herself, slamming the door on the thought. Do not think about Derrick!

She sighed wearily. Her feelings for the man must be stronger than she'd first realized, because she'd closed the door on thoughts of him dozens and dozens of times over the past couple of weeks. But somehow the entrance to her memory of him kept inching open.

Having Timmy in her class made it especially hard to drive Derrick from her mind. She saw the child every weekday, heard him talk about his doings with Derrick. It was agony for her.

Resting her elbow on the desktop, her chin in the palm of her hand, Anna closed her eyelids. Who was she kidding? She couldn't believe she was actually sitting here trying to blame her misery on a little boy when she knew very well that prying Derrick Cheney from her mind would be impossible whether Timmy was one of her students or not.

The sound of loud voices drew her attention to the free play area at the opposite corner of the room. The rainy day had forced the children to take their recess period inside, so she expected lots of noise and laughter. But the very atmosphere at the other end of the room had taken an angry turn. And Timmy was right in the middle of the ruckus.

Timmy was about to get himself into trouble. Anna hoped he wouldn't, but she had seen his behavior over the course of the day growing more and more out of control.

"I said come over here," Timmy demanded of Eric. "Right now!"

"I'm playin' a game of checkers," Eric complained.

Anna could tell Eric was a bit baffled by Timmy's argumentative tone.

"He's playin' with me right now," Andrew said.

Andrew was thin, his complexion sallow, but his frail appearance was misleading. Anna knew he could give as good as he got when he was challenged by a peer.

"Boys," Anna called, getting their attention, "we need to remember to use quiet voices. There are other classes in session, you know."

Seeing April hurry toward the verbal altercation, Anna marveled once again at the psychological dynamics at work within her group of twenty-eight students.

"I'll play a game with you, Timmy," April suggested.

Anna suppressed a warm smile. *That little girl's going to end up being some sort of diplomat,* she thought, and she forced her attention to the spelling papers she'd been grading.

A flurry of violent movement and words had Anna out of her seat in an instant.

"Boys!" she called sharply as she marched toward the back of the room where Andrew and Timmy were engaged in a shoving match.

She reached out and pulled the two boys apart. The entire class of curious children gathered around to see what was happening.

"What is going on here?" she asked.

The boys grew still and silent, but she could feel the anger radiating from both of them. Glancing around her, the scattered red and black plastic discs from the checker game answered some of her question.

"Did you do this?" She directed her question at Timmy.

He jutted out his chin defiantly, but didn't answer.

Anna gazed across the game board to where Eric sat, his eyes wide with fearful excitement. Then she turned her attention to poor, miserable April.

"Why is April crying?" Anna asked.

Keeping the boys spread arm's length apart, she asked the little girl, "Are you hurt, sweetheart?"

Her tiny chin trembled and she pointed an accusing finger at Timmy. "Miss Maxwell, he called me a *girl,*" she said.

The derisive manner in which April spoke the last word, made it clear to Anna that the child was mimicking Timmy's tone when he'd spouted out what he'd thought was a gender slur. And Anna guessed it was a slur, if April took it that way and was hurt by what Timmy said.

"Well, April, you *are* a girl," Anna pointed out with calm practicality. "And there's nothing at all wrong with being a girl. *I'm* a girl." Then she said to clarify, "A female. And half the people on the planet are female."

She could tell from the expression on April's face that the little girl was listening intently. Her tears had stopped, but there was still a deep frown between her brows.

Anna felt more needed to be said to all of these children to eradicate the male chauvinism that had just shown itself.

"Girls are just as smart as boys, you know," she told them. "And we're just as capable as boys, too." She looked at April. "It's nice being a girl."

April was feeling better, Anna could see that.

Suddenly the little girl piped up, "And we're pretty, too."

Fighting hard to hold back the chuckle that threatened to erupt from her throat, Anna let the statement go. Normally, she might have given a small speech against narcissism, but she knew it was more important at the moment for April to regain some of her lost dignity.

"You know, Timmy," Anna said, "it wasn't nice to hurt April's feelings."

Timmy's eyes narrowed, his little body still rigid with anger. "I'm not playin' with no girl."

Anna's brows rose at the disdain in his tone. Because she'd seen him playing with the girls in the class before, she knew the hateful words came solely from the anger and frustration he was feeling about the situation with Eric.

"I'm not playing with any girl," she corrected. "Anger isn't an excuse to use poor English."

She released her hold on Andrew and turned Timmy around so she could talk to him, face-to-face.

"Did you interrupt the checker game?" she asked.

"Andrew was takin' Eric away from me." Timmy nearly shouted the accusation. "If Andrew hadn't set up that stupid checker game, Eric would have been able to—"

"Stop right there," she interrupted. "Eric is your friend. You know that. Andrew is your friend, too. I've seen you play with him. But Eric and Andrew like each other. And they have a right to be friends." She let one of her hands drop to her side. "Besides, Eric has a mind of his own. I heard him tell you that he was playing a game of checkers."

"But Andrew—"

"Enough," she said. "Pushing and shoving is wrong. Both you and Andrew will spend the rest of recess period at your desks." Then she added, "After you've picked up the checkers."

"I won't!" Timmy nearly shouted.

His sharp tone took Anna aback.

"Excuse me, young man?"

"I don't want to do it," Timmy said. "So I don't have to do it."

"That's fine." Anna kept her tone calm, yet authoritative. "April, will you help Eric and Andrew pick up the checkers?"

"Yes, ma'am."

Anna ushered Timmy to his desk, pulled out his

chair and stood there until he sat down. She bent her knees and rested her forearm on Timmy's desk.

"I'm going to have to call home about this, Timmy," she informed him. "I can't have you hurting others and fighting. I can't allow you to defy me. You can't act like that in our classroom." Then she repeated softly, "I'm going to have to call home."

"That's okay," Timmy said. "Uncle Derrick will be on my side."

Anna couldn't stop the worried frown that bit into her brow. "I'm on your side," she told him. "But, Timmy, I have to be on everybody's side." She sighed. "And sometimes that isn't easy. But you were clearly wrong in what you did. And you need to sit here and think about that."

Chapter Five

Anna paced the small confines of the school's front office. She was alone, the school secretary had gone home, but she could hear Mr. Styes, the school principal, in his own office down the short, inner hallway gathering his things together to leave for the day.

Having called Derrick about Timmy's behavior during her planning period, Anna remembered the alarm in his tone and his quick offer to meet with her—*today*. It was unusual for a parent or guardian to drop everything and come to the school.

He had, however, repeated their meeting place—the school office—a couple of times, and she would have smiled at the memory of it if her apprehension would have allowed her. But it wouldn't. She'd not only made a mental note of the time and place of the appointment, but she'd also jotted the information down on paper. But even if she hadn't written it down, she doubted very much if the anxiety gnawing inside her stomach all afternoon at the thought of meeting with Derrick would have permitted her to forget.

Her telephone conversation with Timmy's godfather had been so different from the one she'd had with Andrew's mother, a woman who had had to be pushed and cajoled into coming in to school. The woman had disregarded her son's fighting, saying, "Boys will be boys." When Anna refused to accept that excuse *or* that attitude, the child's mother grudgingly agreed to meet, but not until early the next week, and not without letting Anna know exactly how inconveniencing the whole ordeal was.

Anna sighed. Derrick's concern for Timmy set him miles above a few of the natural-born parents of her students. She figured that was what made him so...appealing—the fact that he cared so much about the welfare of a child who wasn't actually his son.

Though, if she were to be entirely honest, she'd have to admit there was something else that made the man attractive to her. Something about him that allured her...enticed her—

"Is everything all right, Miss Maxwell?"

Anna nearly jumped out of her skin at the sound of Mr. Styes's voice. She'd been so engrossed in her thoughts about Derrick—again—that she hadn't heard the man approach.

"Yes," she assured him. "I'm meeting with Derrick Cheney at three-thirty."

"Ah, yes," Mr. Styes broke in. "About the shoving match today between Timmy Cheney and Andrew Whitney."

Anna was surprised that he'd heard about the incident so quickly.

"Mrs. Sands talked to me about the matter."

Anna had spoken to the school counselor and asked the woman to set up a session for each of the boys to discuss their behavior. Derrick wouldn't like the idea when he found out, but school policy dictated her actions in this case. Besides, she was certain a conversation with Mrs. Sands would help both Timmy and Andrew to better understand why their physical fighting couldn't be tolerated.

"We can't have that kind of aggressive behavior here at school," Mr. Styes said. "I'm glad to see you're addressing the problem so quickly. It shows just how interested you are in your students."

Compliments from Mr. Styes were few and far between. She would have liked to take a moment to savor his words, but dark questions arose in her mind.

Have I become too interested where Timmy is concerned? she wondered. *Have I overstepped my bounds as his teacher?*

"Have you called Mrs. Whitney?"

The principal's question instantly brightened Anna's mood.

"Yes," she answered. "Yes, I did. And I'm meeting with her early next week."

"Good. Let me know how things go." Mr. Styes moved toward the door, throwing over his shoulder, "Have a nice weekend."

Once she was alone, Anna allowed herself to smile. She hadn't overstepped the boundaries of an educator, she decided. She'd called Derrick with her concerns, yes, but she'd called Mrs. Whitney, too. She'd made an appointment to meet with Derrick, but she'd also forced Andrew's mother to come to school to discuss her son's behavior.

But you didn't meet the Whitneys outside of school,

her dark thoughts reasoned stubbornly. *You didn't spend a glorious Saturday morning sailing on the bay....*

Closing her eyes, Anna leaned heavily against the waist-high counter, bowed her head and pressed her fist firmly to her forehead. Why did those moments she'd spent in Derrick's arms continue to haunt her? Why couldn't she simply put them—and him—out of her mind?

"Hello, Anna."

"Derrick!" Her eyes flew open and she stood away from the counter. Unwittingly she glanced at the big-faced clock on the wall. Precisely three-thirty—she should have known.

"You remembered to meet me at the office, I see."

His charming smile caused her heart to ricochet in her rib cage. Her mouth suddenly felt as dry as aged cotton, and rational thought became puffy dandelion seeds blown about by a stiff breeze.

"I wrote it down," she said, hating the breathless quality of her voice.

"Even if you hadn't—" his eyes held a teasing glint "—I'd have come looking for you."

His tone was as warm and intoxicating as honeyed wine, and Anna found herself wanting to sip at it.

He came close, took her hands in his and said, "I've missed you."

A warning bell jangled in her head. She blinked. *Don't allow yourself to be sucked into this...this... atmosphere of seduction.*

Seduction? That was *much* too strong a word to use to describe what happened whenever she and this man came face-to-face....

But as she looked into Derrick's dark, golden-flecked gaze, she was left wondering.

"How have you been?"

His question was spoken with a soft concern that implied nothing less than a deep, personal intimacy—an intimacy that threatened to take away each and every doubt and fear Anna had about getting close to this man.

Think, Anna! she told herself sternly. *Keep your head together. You have reasons for not allowing yourself to have a relationship with Derrick. Important reasons, of which pain, rejection and humiliation are only a few.*

These sobering thoughts caused her to leave his personal question unanswered. Obviously so. But she squared her shoulders and donned her most professional persona.

"Let's go into the conference room," she said, happy that her tone was cool and evinced none of the turmoil she was feeling. She gently pulled her hands from his grasp. "Can I offer you coffee or tea?"

Derrick frowned. She half expected him to confront her, to blatantly ask her why she'd assumed this stiff, impersonal mask, but he didn't and she couldn't deny feeling relieved.

"I'm fine," was all he said.

She went into the windowless conference room, flipping on the overhead fluorescent light.

"Take a seat," she told him.

She waited until he chose a chair, and then she sat down across from, rather than adjacent to, him. For some reason, Anna felt more comfortable with the entire width of the table between them.

There were unasked questions in his eyes, and she

hoped that's where they stayed. She wanted to keep this conference focused on Timmy; however, she couldn't do that if he insisted on probing her personal feelings.

"I'm glad," Derrick said softly, "we're having a chance to get together and talk—"

"About Timmy," Anna cut in, desperate to stress the focal point of their meeting.

His brow creased. "Of course."

Derrick looked toward a corner of the room behind her, and when his gaze once more locked onto her face, the air in the room seemed to have changed its molecular structure, becoming heavy with an undercurrent of thick emotion.

"I was going to call you," he said.

His words were laced with a quiet, tantalizing allure that sent her heart racing. And the expression in his eyes... She swallowed with difficulty. Lord, was it possible for this man to seduce her with something as simple as his tone of voice? Could he enthrall her with mere looks?

"Oh, Derrick," she whispered. Unable to continue to face the intensity in his dark eyes, she looked down at where her hands were clamped together on the conference tabletop. "I just don't think that's a good idea."

She continued to avoid his gaze. The silence that filled the next few moments didn't surprise her, but his next statement did.

"But you told me to."

Lifting her eyes to his, she saw that his frown had deepened. She managed another small, tight swallow.

"I told you to call me if you had a problem with Timmy," she said.

He raised his dark brows a fraction. "Precisely."

"You're having a problem with Timmy?"

He nodded slowly, and Anna felt the heat of embarrassment flush her cheeks. Perspiration prickled her forehead and upper lip, and she fought the urge to wipe her fingertips across her mouth.

Had she totally misread the heavy, seductive atmosphere she'd thought he'd conjured in the room? Had she misinterpreted the enticement in his tone? The invitation in his expression?

She drew her bottom lip between her teeth. Had she made a complete and utter fool of herself here?

There was a knock at the conference room door and then it was pushed open.

"Hello-o-o."

Anna stood and hurried to the door, feeling that she'd never loved the sound of Mrs. Sands's lyrical voice more than she did right now.

"Come in," she said, a wide grin spread across her mouth.

Holding open the door, she ushered the woman into the room.

"Derrick Cheney," Anna said, "this is Mrs. Sands, our school counselor."

He stood and shook hands with the heavyset woman.

"Nice to meet you, Mr. Cheney," Mrs. Sands said.

"I'd like to be able to say the same—" Derrick eased himself warily back down into the seat "—but I must admit that I feel as though you two are about to gang up on me."

He shot a narrowed, questioning glance at Anna.

"Oh, don't feel that way," Mrs. Sands said. "Anna didn't even know I was coming. I ran into Mr. Styes on his way out of the building, and he told me the two of you were meeting. I thought I'd just slip in and say hello, but if you'd rather conduct this meeting without my input—''

"We'd love your input," Anna rushed to assure her, closing the door behind the woman. "Please, sit down with us. Derrick...or rather, Mr. Cheney was just about to tell me about a problem Timmy's having at home."

Mrs. Sands's commanding nature was legendary in the school. She sat down at the head of the conference table and leaned forward on her dimpled elbows, as though she had every intention of taking over the conference. Normally Anna might have felt a little miffed about the counselor's dominant behavior, especially since Mrs. Sands hadn't had the chance to even meet Timmy yet. But Anna was so relieved to have the woman's company that she didn't really mind stepping back and allowing her to take the helm.

"So," Mrs. Sands began, "Timmy's troubles aren't just at school, he's having problems at home, too. That's a significant coincidence, don't you think?"

Anna didn't know if the counselor was addressing her or Derrick, but she could see that Derrick didn't like her question at all.

He, too, leaned forward and rested his elbows on the tabletop. "Tell me," he said, his words holding a grave note, "how did you come to be involved in this?"

The musical quality of Mrs. Sands's voice didn't hide the fact that she took her job seriously. "Mr. Cheney, as part of the Special Education Task Force here at—''

Derrick stood. "I've heard enough."

"It's not what you think," Anna said, her tone loud and rushed. "Please, Derrick, sit down and listen. Mrs. Sands is just a counselor. A school counselor who talks to the children. It's school policy to alert her if there are any physical altercations between students. I've set up a session—one session—for Timmy, during which Mrs. Sands will explain school policy regarding fighting."

Derrick's dark eyes glittered with animosity, and Anna was afraid he'd walk out of the meeting.

"Please, Derrick," Anna pleaded. "Explain your problem. Listen to what she has to say. Let her help you. She's a trained counselor."

He seemed to debate the situation. But finally he lowered himself back into the chair.

"I don't know what that was all about," Mrs. Sands said, "but I really do care about the students attending this school and I do want to help if I can."

Anna was relieved to hear the counselor's tone soften, and she was further pleased when Mrs. Sands relaxed against the back of her chair in a less dominating demeanor. Anna guessed the woman was smart enough to have realized that Derrick wasn't a man to be bullied.

"So," Anna said softly, "tell us what's going on with Timmy at home."

He sighed heavily, then he looked directly across the table at her. "As you know, Tim and I came up with a list of chores for him to do."

"Learning responsibility," Mrs. Sands said quietly, almost to herself. "That's a good thing."

Derrick didn't acknowledge her. "Well, it was going great. And then all of a sudden Tim decided he didn't want to help out around the house any longer."

Anna frowned. She couldn't quite understand Timmy's behavior. She'd believed that feeling needed would be the solution to his problem. She'd witnessed

the child's puppylike eagerness to help Derrick that
Saturday. But now she was stumped.

"May I ask a question?"

Both Anna and Derrick directed their attention to
Mrs. Sands.

"Please," Derrick said tightly.

"What was your reaction to Timmy's refusal?"

"The boy's six years old," he said, as though that
explained everything. Then he shrugged. "I did the
chores myself."

The counselor chuckled. "And you fell right into the
little trap he set up."

Anna watched as Derrick's shoulders squared defen-
sively. "I beg your pardon? What is that supposed to
mean?"

"I'm saying," Mrs. Sands remarked, "that Timmy
manipulated you and you allowed it to happen."

His jaw tensed. His tone increased in volume as he
said, "I don't believe I'm—"

"Let's all calm down a bit," Anna suggested quietly. After they both visibly relaxed, she looked at Mrs.
Sands. "I'm interested to know what you mean."

The woman reached up and lightly scratched a spot
on her chin. "I read Timmy's file. And Andrew Whitney's. I hope you don't mind, but if I'm to meet with
the boys, I thought I'd need to know all I could."

"Oh, I agree," Anna said.

"From the notes you wrote in the child's file," she
said, "I read that Timmy's father was in the Navy. That
Timmy was shuffled from house to house. Not a very
stable environment."

Mrs. Sands directed her gaze at Derrick.

"I also read that you had a career in the Navy, Mr.
Cheney. A career that you gave up in order to raise

Timmy in more solid surroundings, a more secure environment. That's extremely commendable.'' She smiled at him. ''But unfortunately he's testing you.''

''Testing me?'' Derrick's question was spoken in a bewildered whisper.

Mrs. Sands nodded. ''Not consciously, of course. But he *is* testing you. He's testing your resolve. He doesn't think you mean to stick with him.''

''That's so sad,'' Anna remarked.

The counselor shrugged. ''Why would he think otherwise? His father didn't stick with him. His father went out on long tours of duty, leaving him in the care of whoever would take him.'' Then her tone softened. ''Timmy's file tells a very sad story.''

There was a moment of thick silence.

Finally Derrick said, ''But I mean to stick with him.''

''That's good,'' Mrs. Sands said. ''Now all you have to do is let him know that.''

''How?'' he asked.

The woman grinned, a dimple appearing in her rounded cheek. ''One day at a time.''

''Wait a minute,'' he said. ''I need more detailed instructions.''

''Well, for one thing,'' Mrs. Sands said, ''you need to take charge of your home.''

Derrick frowned, and Anna could clearly see he didn't understand, although she knew instantly what the counselor was trying to say.

''Derrick,'' Anna said softly, ''what would have happened when you were in the Navy if the man who was supposed to steer the ship decided he didn't feel like showing up for work?''

''That's a pretty scary thought.''

Anna went on. "Well, would his superior officer have allowed him to shirk his responsibilities?"

"Oh, no," he said. "He'd be disciplined, all right."

"So, there's your answer—" she smiled "—Timmy needs to do his chores to learn responsibility and to feel like a necessary part of the family unit. If he doesn't do them, he needs to be disciplined."

Derrick stared at her, doubt painted a storm cloud across his handsome features.

"I don't know," he said. "This parenting stuff is so much more complicated than I'd first thought. I'm not sure I can do this."

"Of course you can." Anna reached across the table, and without a second thought, without the least sense of self-consciousness, she touched his hand. "Just be firm and loving and you can't go wrong."

Mrs. Sands chuckled. "I hope you're listening to your own advice. Because Timmy's testing you, too."

Anna allowed a small grin to pull at one corner of her mouth. "I know, and I'll take my own advice."

Derrick turned his hand over and took her fingers in his. "Again, I want to thank you."

His cocoa-colored eyes were as somber as she'd ever seen them. She gave him a smile of reassurance and squeezed his hand.

"And you, too, Mrs. Sands," he said. He sighed heavily. "I'm fast learning that I *still* have a lot to learn."

Anna gripped the handle of the canvas bag she used to haul home her planning book and all of her students' papers that needed correcting. She hitched up the shoulder strap of her small leather purse as she walked toward the teachers' parking lot.

All in all, she'd have to say that her conference with Derrick had gone well. There had been a moment of extreme awkwardness—a moment early on when she'd thought she'd read a deep intimacy in Derrick's voice, in his gaze, in his very expression. But luckily **Mrs.** Sands had joined the meeting and a precarious and uncomfortable situation had been avoided by the woman's presence. And she'd been relieved to escape further awkward circumstances when Derrick had left the meeting after the school counselor requested to speak with her concerning the other child involved in the fight, Andrew Whitney.

Anna bent to insert the key in the door lock.

"Anna."

Turning at the sound of Derrick's voice, she felt her heart skip a beat at the sight of him about ten feet from her.

"I didn't want to startle you," he said, coming closer.

An appreciative smile tugged at her lips. "Thanks," she murmured.

It was amazing to her how, every time she met this man, she succeeded in presenting a calm exterior, when all the while her insides were running riot. This time was no exception; her heart pounded, her nerves came alive, even her skin began to tingle. However, she was able to offer him a spontaneous, relaxed smile even though a sudden apprehension filled her stomach with a thousand buzzing bees.

"Can we talk?" he asked. "I'll only keep you a minute, but…there are some things I need to say."

Once again Anna felt trapped in the eye of the high-speed tornado that always seemed to twirl and twist around the two of them when they were together. The central spot of this emotional storm was invariably an airless vacuum in which she found it impossible to breathe.

Unable to utter a word, she simply studied his face and hoped she looked more in control than she felt.

"Yes, I was going to call you about my problems with Tim," he said softly. "But I had every intention of speaking to you about something else. Something personal." He hesitated only a moment. "Us."

There was an unspoken request in his dark, velvety eyes, a silent petition that she not interrupt him, that she allow him to have his say. Anna granted his request, not because she wanted to hear these "personal" thoughts he wanted to voice, but because she simply couldn't find the strength to stop him.

She should stop him. She should. That was so very obvious to her. But she just couldn't.

"Listen," he said. "I know you're a special teacher. You've proved that to me by the way you care about Tim. And the other children in your class."

He shifted his weight from one foot to the other, and Anna sensed that he was going to reach out to her.

Please don't touch me, she said silently. *Please don't.*

Derrick gently placed his warm fingers on her forearm, and surprisingly, the contact caused a calming hum to radiate across her skin. Her heart rate seemed to steady, her blood ceased to pound in her ears.

"But you're a special person, too."

A heated curl of pleasure sprouted inside her at his compliment.

"A very special person."

His voice took on a nectar-sweet thickness, an intimate huskiness meant only for her ears. The rich res-

onance and texture of his expression wholly overwhelmed her—so did the meaning of the wonderful
words he was saying.

He went on. "And I think that, even from that small
amount of time we spent together on the boat, there's
something special between you and me."

That brown gaze of his darkened to a deep mahogany. "Something I think we really need to explore."

She knew she should step away from him, at least
far enough so that she no longer felt his skin on hers.
But even as the thought entered her head, he slid his
fingers across her forearm, curled them over the curve
of her arm and held on, almost as if he knew she meant
to escape.

"I've felt," he continued, "ever since we were out
on the bay, that you've been running from me." His
mouth tipped up into a soft smile. "But I refuse to
allow you to get away until we've discovered what
this…something is."

Her brain absorbed his last statement. Here's your
chance! it told her. You can deny feeling this special
something he's talking about. You can act cool, calm
and collected, and flat-out lie about the specialness, the
electricity, the emotional storm that sweeps over you
every time you're in his company. Heck, every time
you even think about him!

She swallowed. But would that be fair to him? a tiny
voice inside her asked.

Anna looked down at the pavement. She bent her
knees just enough so that she could set down the canvas bag at her feet to give herself a few moments.

Time. She desperately needed time to think this
through. But time wasn't something she had a lot of

right now. Derrick was standing here in front of her expecting her to say...something.

A furious battle took place in her head as the next few seconds flew by. A battle in which her protective instinct fought with the part of her that wanted to be honest, upright and true.

She needed protecting, that was certain. She wanted desperately to avoid the humiliation she knew she would see in his dark eyes if he knew the full truth. But did that mean she had to lie about how she felt? Did that mean she had to deceive him by acting as though she were blind to what *he already knew* was staring them both right in the face?

Raising her eyes to his, she absently drew her tongue across her lips to moisten them before she spoke. She lifted her free hand and placed her flattened palm against the front of his soft cotton dress shirt.

"Derrick," she began, "I won't deny that there's... there's—" she shook her head helplessly as she searched for some descriptive word to define the churning, pulsing emotions she felt "—*something* here between us. I don't know if it's some weird kind of chemistry...or some deep attraction—"

He chuckled, and the smile he gave her in response to her attempt to define this "thing" was nearly wicked, and she felt an intense urge to return it. But she didn't. Because she knew he wasn't going to like the rest of what she had to say.

Again she licked her lips and steeled herself to finish.

"But we can't explore it," she said.

His smile faded, and in her mind she seemed to stumble over the words she'd meant to say.

Suddenly she tipped up her chin a fraction. This was no time to falter.

"I can't allow that," she told him, and she was pleased that her statement had come out sounding so firm and yet gentle. "And I can't give you an explanation."

She blinked once, twice. "All I can tell you...is that it wouldn't work."

Her hand slid from his chest, and she reached down to pick up her bag from the ground. She stepped away from the car, pulled open the door and placed the bag on the center of the front seat. She was relieved that he did nothing to stop her.

She straightened and turned back to him.

"You'll have to trust me on this."

After speaking those last few words, she slid behind the wheel, started the engine and pulled away.

Anna turned onto the main road, not daring to look in her rearview mirror. She placed her hand high on the left side of her rib cage, hoping that he wasn't feeling the same kind of ripping and tearing in his heart as she was feeling in hers.

Chapter Six

Derrick stood at the kitchen sink and scraped the skins from the carrots into the food disposal. The first time he'd used the vegetable peeler, he'd flayed the top layer of flesh from the entire length of his thumb. He was pleased to realize that his technique and skill had improved with months of practice and he could now use the utensil without drawing blood.

When he'd been in the Navy, he'd only had to go to the nearest Officer's Club to get himself a decent meal. But now as a civilian he'd had to learn to read recipes, measure ingredients, peel, chop, season, simmer, braise, fry and bake. He'd discovered a whole new world that included leavening agents and food additives such as herbs and spices that affected the taste, texture and nutritive value of the meals he prepared. He was an accountant, for goodness sake, not a chemist. And probably the hardest part of cooking had been learning to time the process so that all the food was finished at the same time. He chuckled, remembering the dried-out hamburgers and roasts that he and Timmy had eaten with potatoes that weren't quite done. However, he'd been determined to master the skill of cooking and now he felt quite at home in the kitchen.

In fact, he'd now become so adept at peeling and chopping vegetables that while he was performing the task, he felt comfortable enough to allow himself to remember his last moments with Anna today in the school parking lot.

She'd agreed that there was something special in the air when the two of them were together. Yet she'd refused his suggestion that they explore what they felt for each other.

Lord, he didn't know what it was he felt for Anna, all he did know was that the kiss they shared on the boat that Saturday morning had rocked his senses. She'd made him feel the way no other woman had.

But she'd been adamant that a relationship between them would never work. He couldn't help but wonder what her reasons had been for making such a strong statement.

As he rinsed the carrots, one by one, and placed them on a paper towel, he decided that he shouldn't worry over something he couldn't do much about at the moment. Right now he needed to focus all his attention on Timmy. With that in mind he began to mull over some of the things Anna and the school counselor had said to him that afternoon about his godson.

The thing that bothered him the most was Mrs. Sands's suggestion that Tim didn't believe Derrick was going to stick with him. He hated to think that his godson felt insecure about this new family the two of them were developing. And he still felt frustrated by the counselor's advice that the solution lay in a ''one day at a time'' approach. The problem solver inside him wanted to come up with a quick and easy solution that would ease Timmy's mind.

Derrick also didn't like the idea that Tim was being manipulative. If he was learning to exploit authority at the young age of six, what would that lead to later on in his life? Derrick wondered. It frightened him to realize that every answer to that question that crossed his mind didn't point to a healthy, ambitious adult life for Tim.

Authority. Somehow that seemed to be a key word here.

Derrick was finding out that he'd become Tim's guardian thinking it was going to be a buddy system of sorts. A fun time during which he and Tim would go sailing or to ball games. But Derrick had quickly come to understand that Tim was constantly learning, that Tim's every waking moment was spent acquiring the skills to be a competent person. And Derrick was only now coming to understand that he was one of Tim's teachers in this ''life lesson.''

As he sliced the carrots into small rounds, the magnitude of the job of raising Tim seemed suddenly overwhelming to him.

He couldn't be Tim's buddy, he couldn't be his friend—not if he was going to be the authority figure in the boy's life. And that was just what Derrick needed to be, now that Timmy had begun testing authority.

''Use firm and loving discipline.'' Anna's soft, feminine voice flitted through his head, and Derrick felt less alone.

Firm and loving discipline. The idea was a good one, he knew. It came from the experts—teachers and counselors. But how was he to discipline a child like Tim?

Taking television away from the boy was useless because Tim watched so little of it. Derrick chuckled suddenly, thinking maybe he should force Tim to sit and watch several of those nonsensical game shows or a couple hours of tabloid television. No, he shook his head. That would be torturous child abuse.

Derrick couldn't take away outside playtime. Tim really didn't play outdoors much.

Tim did spend a great deal of time reading. But Derrick couldn't very well take away the child's books.

He dumped the carrots and the potatoes he'd already cubed into the pot of simmering beef stew and set the timer on the stove for fifteen minutes.

Opening the cabinet, he pulled down salad plates and bowls for the stew and turned toward the table. Then he stopped.

Setting the table was one of Tim's chores—one of the chores that, for the past few days, he'd refused to do. The thought prompted Derrick to set the dishes down on the kitchen counter and go down the hallway toward the bedrooms to look for Tim.

He knocked on the closed door.

"Yes?" Tim answered.

Derrick opened the door, leaned into the room and saw his godson sprawled out on the twin bed, leafing through a book. "It's time for you to set the table for dinner," he said.

"Aw, but...I already told you," Timmy said in a whiny voice, "I don't feel like doin' that anymore."

Apprehension solidified in the pit of Derrick's gut as heavy as a concrete block. In all his years as an officer in the United States Navy, he'd never felt the least bit anxious about doling out discipline when it was deserved. But now the turmoil that roiled inside him as he thought about correcting his godson made him feel as though he were nearly in a panic.

"Just be firm and loving." He could hear Anna's voice silently coaching him.

"Well, Tim," he said, "it's on your list of chores. You agreed to do it when we sat down together and made the list."

"But—"

Derrick's raised brows stopped whatever excuse Timmy had been about to give. "This isn't a request," he said, his tone quiet yet firm.

Timmy hesitated, as though he was considering his options. Finally his little chin tipped upward. "But I really don't wanna right now."

The defiance in the boy's tone surprised Derrick, and he realized immediately that this childish tactic was part of the testing and manipulation that Mrs. Sands had mentioned. He worked hard to contain his irritation, reminding himself that Tim was only six, that the school counselor had told him that this behavior was not conscious and was caused by the insecurity the boy was feeling.

"Well," Derrick said, keeping his tone even and sincere, "I can only hope you'll come and do the job. Because if you don't, you'll only be adding to the punishment you already have coming."

With that said, he gently closed the door and turned to go back down the hallway toward the kitchen.

As he expected, the door sprang open quickly and Timmy was soon following close on his heels.

"Punishment?" the boy said. "For what?"

"For your behavior in school today," Derrick informed him.

"But Andrew was fighting, too!"

Turning the corner into the kitchen, Derrick went to the stove to check on dinner.

"And I didn't start it! It was all Andrew's fault."

Calmness suddenly lightened the heavy anxiety that had been weighing on him back in Tim's bedroom. This immature behavior was an act of desperation to avoid punishment, and that knowledge helped Derrick to put everything into perspective. No, the child hadn't committed murder, but Derrick couldn't allow Tim to go against school rules and get away with it. Neither could he allow him to lie.

"You know very well," he said softly, "that I spoke to your teacher today, and I think you're not being entirely truthful about who's to blame."

Timmy ducked his head, went to the counter and plucked up the dishes that Derrick had placed there.

Derrick bent over the pot of simmering stew and stirred it, suppressing a smile. He was glad that he hadn't had to press the issue of Tim setting the table for dinner.

When the boy stalked to the silverware drawer and angrily jerked it open, Derrick forced himself not to react.

"It's Miss Maxwell's fault," Timmy muttered. "She tried to make me pick up the checkers."

"Who lost his temper and flung the checkers all over the play area?"

Derrick went to the table and busied himself folding the paper napkins into triangles as he covertly studied Timmy's face. The boy's chin began to tremble the slightest bit as he placed the cutlery beside the plates.

"It doesn't matter," Tim blurted all of a sudden. "This'll pass."

The emotion that swept over Derrick at hearing those

words made him weak in the knees. Timmy's father had said those very words so many times.

"This will pass," James would say, if he had to pull a tour of duty he disliked. It had been James's motto— a phrase to help get him through the bad times in his life. Derrick remembered his cousin chanting those three little words over and over during the weeks following the accident that took Timmy's mother's life.

Derrick eased himself down into the hard-backed chair. "Yes, Tim, this *will* pass. But it's not true when you say it doesn't matter. Because it does. It matters a lot. We have to learn something from this. And we can't learn anything unless we remember it." He reached out and touched Timmy on the shoulder. "Do you understand? We have to learn from our mistakes."

The boy shrugged. "What's to learn?" he asked.

"Sit down," he told Tim. "Listen to me. You are responsible for your actions. You were involved in a fight today—"

"But Andrew—"

He stopped Timmy with a stern expression. "I understand that Andrew was also involved," he said gently. "I can't concern myself with how his parents choose to deal with the problem. All I can do is be certain that you learn from this incident. You have to understand that you are responsible for everything that you say and everything that you do."

The boy lowered his gaze and stared at the empty salad plate in front of him.

"Fighting is against the school rules," Derrick said. "You'll be meeting with the school's counselor next week to go over what constitutes good and bad behavior." He paused for a moment. "But I think, deep down in your heart, you know what you did today was wrong. There isn't a reason good enough to excuse what you did.''

Timmy's rounded shoulders told Derrick that his message was understood. The boy refused to look at him, and Derrick felt the urge to give in, hug the child and forgive everything. But he knew he wouldn't be teaching Tim anything if he did. So now was the time to dole out the punishment.

''Firm and loving.'' He heard a gentle voice and almost smiled.

''Remember how I said that in order to learn from our mistakes we have to remember them?'' Derrick quietly asked.

Tim cast him a shy glance. ''Yes, sir.''

''Well, to help you remember this bad behavior, I want you to get up bright and early tomorrow morning, go into the garage and start preparing all the recyclables.''

''But—''

Derrick stopped him with an upraised index finger. ''I want you to rinse out all the plastic bottles and bag them up. The steel cans need to have the labels removed, and all the aluminum cans need to be crushed and bagged.''

Timmy swallowed, his eyes wide. ''But there's a month's worth of stuff in the bins.''

''I know,'' Derrick said. ''It's a big job, but I think you can handle it.''

''It's gonna take me forever.''

Derrick chuckled. ''No,'' he said. ''But it will take you most of tomorrow.'' He squeezed Timmy's arm reassuringly. ''And tomorrow evening, when you're all through, we'll go to the recycling center.''

He stood and went to the stove. After taking the lid

from the pot, he began ladling the thick, steaming stew into a serving bowl.

"Grab the salad from the fridge, would you?" he asked Tim.

Setting the bowl of stew on the table, Derrick said, "Oh, and by the way, your work in the garage doesn't relieve you of your normal Saturday chores. You still have to find the time to clean your room and take out the garbage."

Timmy's mouth set into a straight, angry line.

"You have to remember," Derrick said, "it was your behavior that has caused you this extra work." He couldn't help the tiny smile that tugged at his mouth. "You can take out all of your aggressions when you crush those aluminum cans tomorrow."

Silently the boy slid into his seat, his chin practically touching his chest. It was a sight that ripped at Derrick's heart. He wanted so badly to pull the child to him, to alleviate all of his anxieties, but he knew that now wasn't the time to do it. Tim had a lesson to learn, and a big part of that lesson was to think about what he'd done and realize that his behavior was improper. If Derrick were to give in now, all of the groundwork he'd just laid would be for naught.

He sat at the table and served himself some crisp salad greens before passing the bowl to his godson.

Derrick pictured his actions tomorrow afternoon when he and Tim went to the recycling center. That would be the most opportune time for him to compliment the boy on a job well done. To hug him and tell him how proud he felt. That would be the perfect time to talk about the fight at school, after Tim had spent the day thinking about his part in the whole matter.

Yes, tomorrow would be a milestone event in this

new family relationship the two of them were developing.

But as Derrick munched on a crunchy bite of cucumber, he wanted badly to lighten the heavy mood that seemed to blanket the entire house. A little reassurance couldn't hurt, he thought.

He reached out and patted Tim's hand.

"Hey," he said. "We're in this together, you and me. We're in this for the long haul."

Derrick realized that Tim didn't understand the deep, loving message he was trying to send.

But I'll make you understand eventually, he silently vowed. I'll make you see that I mean to stick by you, that I love you. I'll earn your trust. Day by day.

The mid-afternoon, autumnal sun was casting slanted shadows from the trees in the schoolyard. Derrick paced back and forth in front of the entrance to the brick building. He was filled with conflicting emotions—emotions that had his insides churning.

The elation he'd felt ever since Saturday afternoon had never left him. His conversation with Timmy couldn't have gone better. After completing the job he'd been given, the child had freely talked about what he had been feeling when he'd picked a fight with Andrew. Tim had been heart-wrenchingly honest about the jealousy he'd felt over Andrew playing with Eric. When Derrick had suggested Tim apologize to Andrew and Eric for what he'd done, the boy had surprisingly gone one step further, saying he also needed to apologize to April, a little girl in his class whose feelings he'd hurt, and to Miss Maxwell for his refusal to pick up the checkers as she'd asked him to do.

Derrick felt as though he'd succeeded in his first

"fatherly" act of doling out punishment. And it was all because of Anna's advice.

"Just be firm and loving," she'd said. And that bit of wisdom was exactly what he accredited his success to.

All weekend he'd wanted to talk to Anna, to share with her all the things he was going through with Timmy. But he hadn't been able to do that. He didn't know how to contact her except through the school. And he'd remembered overhearing Anna tell the school counselor that she'd be meeting with Andrew Whitney's mother this afternoon.

So, here it was Monday, and he was filled to the brim with this exciting news and the wild desire to share it with Anna. And he planned to do just that as soon as she was finished her conference with Mrs. Whitney.

But as much as the success concerning his weekend with Timmy had him feeling wonderfully ecstatic, he also had to admit that a part of him was feeling unsure and even anxious about seeing Anna. The woman had told him she had no interest in seeing him on a personal level. He should respect that.

"And I will," he told himself aloud. "Absolutely."

Just as a dark part of his brain was about to question the sincerity of his spoken statement, a prudish-looking woman came marching from the school.

Derrick nodded a greeting, but the woman, whom he suspected to be Mrs. Whitney, barely noticed him in her haste to leave the school premises.

As he stood at the door debating whether to go looking for Anna or to simply wait for her to leave the school, he was nearly struck by the heavy wood and glass door as she exited.

"Oh," she cried, scrambling to keep her armload of art supplies from tumbling from her grasp. "I'm sorry."

"It's okay," Derrick rushed to assure her. "I'm not hurt."

"Derrick!" She stared at him, wide-eyed and waiting.

She looked so beautiful when she was startled, he thought. It was so obvious to him that he was the last person she was expecting to see.

The soft, black sweater she wore was a bit sedate for her usual tastes, he noticed, but she made up for it with the scarf and matching skirt that were color blocked with vivid primary colors. The green in the scarf complemented her eyes perfectly.

A gentle October breeze blew her full, black hair across her face, and he had to force himself not to reach out and brush it back. The breath of air died quickly and left the two of them gazing at each other in total silence.

Suddenly he felt as though his tongue were glued to the roof of his mouth. He could think of absolutely nothing to say. And for a split second he couldn't even remember why he'd come.

The bottoms of her high-heeled shoes scraped on the cement walkway as she shifted her position.

"I left my canvas bag at home this morning," she told him.

His heart raced at the melodious sound of her voice. It was almost as though his auditory senses had been deprived and this was the first sound he'd heard in ages. He couldn't help but think the idea was a weird one, but it passed through his mind nonetheless.

She laughed self-consciously. "I think I'd leave my

head at home if it wasn't conveniently attached to my shoulders.''

And what beautiful, shapely shoulders they are, too, he thought. He allowed his eyes to rove from her face, down the long length of her milk white neck to her shoulders.

He wanted badly to reach out and smooth his fingertips over the soft knitted fabric of the black sweater that covered her shoulders. Then, unwittingly, his eyes dipped a few inches lower, but his view was cut off by the plastic bottles of premixed paint, fat, white-bristled brushes and a stack of multicolored construction paper.

"Derrick."

Instantly his gaze was once again riveted to her face. He felt slightly embarrassed that she'd had to call out his name to garner his attention like he was one of her six-year-old first-grade students.

Wasn't *she* the one who was normally a little on the forgetful side? Wasn't *she* the one whose attention could so easily be diverted by the least distraction? What on earth was wrong with him?

"I wanted to try a new art project with the children tomorrow."

Her tone was light, almost forced, as though she was determined to ignore his little indiscretion of openly staring at her body.

"And since I didn't have anything to carry all this home in..."

She indicated the supplies she awkwardly carried in her arms.

Derrick blinked, suddenly feeling ungallant that he hadn't come to her aid more quickly.

"Here," he said, taking several bottles of paint from her arms, "let me help you."

She didn't refuse.

"My car's right over there," she said. "Well, I guess you already know where I park, since you were just in the teacher's parking lot on Friday."

Her mention of their last meeting was a gentle warning, he knew that. And he might even have heeded it—if he were in his right mind. But he wasn't.

"Well—" she hesitated "—let's go."

When she brushed past him, he got a whiff of her perfume—a dark, mysterious fragrance he'd never noticed before. He wondered if she'd been wearing the scent when they had gone sailing together. He was certain she hadn't, because he knew without a doubt that he would have remembered it.

He hurried to catch up with her, and as he walked beside her toward her car, he somehow felt taller, stronger.

Another weird thought, he told himself.

And suddenly, like a lightning bolt from the clear, blue sky above, he was struck with a huge, crystal-clear revelation—a revelation that had his heart doing a jack-knife inside his rib cage. *He wanted this woman!* He wanted to go out with her. Be seen with her. And going even further than that, he realized that he had no intention whatsoever of respecting the fact that Anna had no interest in seeing him on a personal level.

No, Derrick thought as he casually walked next to her toward the parking lot, he hadn't. In fact, he was going to do everything in his power to persuade her go out to dinner with him. Tonight.

Chapter Seven

Anna was on her guard, her internal warning system pulsing like slow-scanning radar. She'd felt the steady, heavy cadence since the instant she'd walked out of the school, nearly striking someone with the door—and finding out that that someone had been Derrick.

She hadn't been ready for him. Her self-preserving instincts hadn't been charged and at the ready, and seeing him had been quite startling.

Her meeting with Andrew Whitney's mother hadn't gone very well. The woman failed to see the serious problems that could result from her refusal to sternly address her son's aggressive behavior. So it was no wonder she hadn't been ready for the flood of emotion that charged through her when she'd first encountered Derrick.

But her guard was up now. And those strong defenses had helped keep her calm and cool even when their eyes had caught and held directly after her surprise had caused her to gasp his name.

During those few silent seconds of staring, she had felt currents of electricity humming across her skin, jolting each and every nerve ending in her body. But she'd held strong. When he couldn't seem to get himself together enough to speak, she'd risen to the occasion quite effectively and come up with some mundane conversation to get them through those first awkward moments. She'd felt quite proud of herself.

They were walking to her car now, and even though she kept her eyes and face in a stiff, forward direction, she sensed the tall, solid mass of him beside her. Why had he come to see her? she wondered.

As she pondered the question, the sudden desire to inch closer to him slithered its way into her consciousness. Her eyes widened the slightest bit, and without slowing her step in the least, she mentally grabbed the urge by the throat and choked the life out of it. She couldn't be entertaining such fantasies. Not after the pains she'd taken on Friday afternoon to let Derrick know that she felt it wouldn't be a good idea for the two of them to see each other on any kind of personal level.

When they reached her car, she unlocked and opened the trunk. She let the plastic bottles of paint she carried roll from her arms and thump into the bottom of the compartment.

This silence from Derrick was so...unusual to witness. The man she had come to know always seemed so self-assured, and she'd found that trait to be very appealing.

She watched as he placed the supplies into her trunk.

But now he seemed...almost shy. She nearly smiled thinking that this big, assertive guy was having trouble expressing himself. She couldn't help but think it was…cute.

The air around them started to sing with some kind of unidentifiable…something. No, she decided, the warble in the atmosphere hadn't just started—she'd been slightly conscious of it ever since she'd exited the school building—but what she noticed was that its volume had all of a sudden increased by several decibels.

Every bit of intuition she possessed shouted for her to be wary and cautious.

She felt that she'd be better able to fight off this… this…*thing* if she could just put a name to it. If she could just identify this…whatever it was that was twisting and tangling itself around the two of them.

Derrick reached up, flattened his palm against the top of the trunk lid and firmly closed it. Then he faced her, a small smile planted on his mouth.

"I do have a good reason for coming to see you."

His statement was spoken with some hesitancy. *And was that…my, heavens, yes,* she thought. *His face was actually tinged with color!*

Anna found his awkwardness so very engaging that her mental aegis unwittingly slipped a fraction of an inch and her lips tipped up in the tiniest of smiles.

"I talked with Tim this weekend," he said, "and I wanted to share my experience with you."

He launched into his story with a great deal of fervor, and Anna saw the Derrick she knew come to life. His voice was filled with happiness and a large measure of success as he talked. His face expressed with animation his pride concerning his first real act of gentle, loving authority. His very stature seemed to increase as his self-confidence reemerged.

"So," he concluded, "I think I handled things pretty

well, and Tim was a real trouper about sticking to the job I gave him as punishment.''

One of his hands rested on the trunk lid, the other, on his hip.

Anna nodded. "Timmy was a changed little boy today," she told him. "He apologized to everyone concerned—'' she touched her fingertips to the base of her throat "—even me. And I overheard him bragging to Eric about the work you made him do."

"Bragging?" His eyebrows inched up in total surprise.

She chuckled lightly. "Yes." She leaned her hip against the back of her car. "You see, children are always testing the boundaries, pushing the limits. They think they want to break loose, when actually they would much prefer to be reined in. It makes them feel safe.''

"So that's what I did, huh? I reined Timmy in?"

"Exactly.''

His dark eyes became serious. "Now that I've kind of taken charge and showed Tim who's at the helm, do you think everything should be smooth sailing from here on out?"

Anna wanted to laugh at his innocence, but she didn't.

"Sure," she said, and he looked visibly relieved. "For about a week…maybe two."

His gaze darted to her face. "What?"

This time she couldn't hold back her laughter. "Derrick, he's a kid. Kids don't test the boundaries once and then let them alone."

"They don't?"

"If there's one sure bet you can make," she said,

"it's that Timmy's going to test you and test you and test you."

Derrick's shoulders sagged just a bit as he digested what she was saying.

Finally he asked, "But doesn't there ever come a time when he knows the boundaries? When he knows the limits and doesn't need to push?"

"Sure. When he's all grown up and ready to move out on his own."

"Oh," Derrick groaned, putting his hand up to the side of his head. "Every time I talk to you about this job I've undertaken, I find out things that make my head swim." He studied her for a moment. "How do you do it?" he asked. "How do you spend each day with two dozen kids and not lose your mind?"

Humor bubbled from her throat, generous and unself-conscious. "I use the same advice I gave you," she told him. "I'm firm and loving. And consistent."

He grinned.

"And you're forgetting," she added. "I get weekends and summers off."

"Oh, so that's how you survive?"

The boyish charm exuding from him reached out to her, teasing her with its unseen tendrils.

He asked, "Who do I see to get weekends and summers off?"

"Sorry ," she said lightly, "but you don't get any time off."

His voice grew softer. "Ever?"

"Ever," she said. A languorous chuckle escaped from deep in her throat. "Didn't they tell you that?"

A curling lock of her hair blew across her cheekbone, and Derrick reached out, taking it between his fingers.

"You're beautiful when you smile," he said huskily, searching her gaze with his dark, velvety eyes.

Anna wanted badly to press her cheek to the backs of his fingers. The thought should have triggered her alarm, alerted her to the fact that he'd somehow scaled the walls of the fortress with which she'd surrounded herself and her emotions. But her alarm wasn't triggered. And the funny thing was she didn't feel the least bit panicked.

She guessed it was inevitable that this soldier would breach every defense she'd built against him. She should feel upset with him for not heeding the message she gave him the last time they were together. She should feel terrifically angry with herself for not keeping a more vigilant watch.

"Anna—" his tone lowered to a most seductive octave "—come out with me. Right now. Let's have dinner."

His request elicited her laughter. "But, Derrick," she said, "it's only four-thirty in the afternoon."

"A cup of coffee, then," he countered. "A walk in the park. I don't care what we do. I just want to spend some time with you."

She let her eyes rove over his features: those intense mahogany eyes, that strong jaw, his angular cheekbones, the military-styled, sandy blond hair, all the purely physical attributes that made up his handsome, clean-cut good looks. She should say no, she knew that. She should not only say no, she should run like hell.

But as she stood there, enveloped in a thick blanket of...whatever it was humming in the air all around her, she simply couldn't say no. So she did the next best thing. She said nothing.

"Now, Anna, I know what you said on Friday. I

know you don't want to get involved. I don't know your reason, I don't want to know your reason."

He gently tucked behind her ear the tendril of her hair he'd been caressing, then he slowly trailed his fingertip down the length of her jaw

"I don't know if you've been hurt in the past or what," he said. "I'm not asking you to become...involved with me. I'm not asking for any kind of permanent relationship here. It's much too soon for that." He took her chin between his index finger and thumb. "I only want to get to know you."

Movement from the corner of her eye had her turning her head away from him. His hand moved away from her face, and she sensed rather than saw him resettle his weight on both feet as a fellow teacher nodded at them.

"Bye, Chuck," Anna called. "Have a nice evening."

The man waved, got into his car and drove away.

The mood should have been broken by the interruption, but when she turned back to face Derrick, she felt just as encompassed by the heavy aura as she had been before.

"What do you say, Anna?" he said. "Let's go somewhere and have a cup of coffee."

He reached out and touched her arm, and Anna felt the heat of his skin through the soft fabric of her sweater. The light pressure of his fingertips on her flesh churned up waves of sensual emotion inside of her. And along with this sensual emotion came the rushing swell of sweet surrender.

"Okay." She heard herself whisper the word at the same instant that she decided she wanted to be with

Derrick, even if it was only to go and have a cup of coffee.

She should have been shocked by the ease with which she yielded to her desire to be with him. She hadn't had to be dragged kicking and screaming, rather it had been more of a gentle succumbing to the inevitable.

It was a bad decision; she realized that deep in her heart. One she would most probably rue. But she would worry about that tomorrow.

He took her elbow, and she allowed him to lead her across the grassy area to the visitors' parking lot.

"I'll bring you back to pick up your car later," he told her.

She could feel his fingers trembling where he grasped her arm, and she darted a quick glance at his face. His eyes were filled with a nervous tension that she found extremely endearing.

Her inhalation was shaky and she realized that she was just as anxious as he.

What on earth were they doing? She had papers to grade, work sheets to prepare. Knowing his accounting firm was so new and growing by leaps and bounds, he was certain to have appointments to keep, clients to talk to. But here they were, sneaking off in the middle of the afternoon.

Derrick opened the passenger door of his car and helped her inside. She watched him round the car, her heart thumping as anticipation washed over her. They were acting like two irresponsible kids, and when he closed his door behind him, she voiced those very words to him.

"Yeah," he said, gunning the engine and putting the car into gear, "we are, aren't we?"

He turned the car onto the main road and headed toward town. "Oh."

The small word broke the silence inside the car and made Anna look his way.

"What?"

"I...um," he stammered, "sort of forgot about Timmy. He's with a sitter. Chrissy. She's a teenager who lives just a few doors down from me. But I didn't expect to be gone very long." He tossed a quick, sheepish look at her before once again watching the road. "You see, this was all pretty...spontaneous. I hadn't planned to...well, I had no idea—"

"It's okay," she assured him. "I know exactly how you feel. Neither one of us planned this." And we could no more have stopped it than we could have stopped a speeding freight train, she added silently.

"I'll call when we get to the coffee shop," he said. "If Chrissy can't stay, then I'll make some other arrangement."

The tiny coffee shop was newly opened and on the main thoroughfare of the small town. At this time in the late afternoon, between lunch and dinner, they had the place nearly to themselves. The waitress seated them in a back, corner booth, and Derrick and Anna smiled at each other.

After the waitress left them to study the menu, Anna whispered, "It's obvious that even she thinks we're sneaking off to be alone. Otherwise, why seat us here in the back of beyond?"

He shot her the most delectable grin. "A clandestine meeting. Sounds kind of erotic, doesn't it?"

Not trusting herself to speak, Anna only smiled. Just being with you is erotic, she thought but didn't dare speak the opinion aloud.

The waitress brought red-checkered linen napkins and fresh silverware.

"I'm sorry the table wasn't set," she told them. "We don't get many customers this time of day." She took a small pad of order slips from the pocket of her starched white apron. "Will you be eating?"

"No," Derrick said. "Just coffee." Then he looked at Anna. "But then, how about a cappuccino?"

"Sounds wonderful."

"Two cappuccinos," the waitress said, and she went off into the kitchen.

"Excuse me just a minute," Derrick said. "I'm going to go call home."

She watched him slip from his seat, and her gaze followed him all the way to the vestibule where he plunked some coins into the public telephone.

Resting her elbow on the tabletop, Anna laced her fingers together. What are you doing? she silently asked herself as her thumbs battled one another. Why are you here when you know it is the worst place in the world for you to be?

She really couldn't find any answers. All she did know was that she'd never in her life felt attracted to a man the way she felt attracted to Derrick. Never in her life had she experienced the…electricity…or the raw magnetism…or whatever it was that affected the very air when he was near.

This wasn't a sane thing for her to be doing. She knew that as well as she knew the English alphabet. But it was something she wanted—something she wanted so badly that she knew it was useless to fight it.

The hurt would come. As surely as the sun would rise tomorrow, she knew what she was doing right now would cause her pain. However, she simply chose not to think about it at this moment. She simply chose to enjoy the here and now.

"Okay," Derrick said as he sat back down across from her, "everything's set. Chrissy's going to stay another couple of hours. She's even going to help Tim with his homework."

"He shouldn't have any problem," Anna told him. "He just needs to practice writing his letters, and he has a coloring work sheet. Oh, and a math sheet. Simple addition."

His dark eyes grew serious. "You really like working with kids, don't you?"

"Very much," she told him. "The most difficult thing about teaching first grade is that each child comes into elementary school at a different level of learning. Some of the kids can't recite the alphabet, yet some of them can already read. Some can't count to ten, while others can do addition and subtraction."

"How do you cope when you have so many different stages at once?" he asked.

Anna rested her clasped hands on the table. "The fun—and exciting—part of my job is keeping everyone challenged. It's not an easy thing, but if I keep on my toes—" one corner of her mouth cocked up in a grin "—I can do an okay job."

"You do a fabulous job," he murmured.

He reached out and ran his fingertip lightly along her forearm. Anna's breath caught in her throat. It was almost as though a spell had been cast over them. And even when the waitress returned to their table and set down the two cups of steaming cappuccino, the captivating bewitchery was not broken.

The waitress hurried off, as though she realized and

was embarrassed that she'd intruded on an intimate moment.

"I want to know everything about you there is to know." His voice was low, and the utterly seductive tone of it caused a shiver of excitement to course along her spine.

"Me, too," she whispered. And then when she realized what she said, she clarified, "About *you*, I mean."

So over the cups of hot, milky coffee, they talked. About their childhoods. About their teenage years. About their college days. And all the while, Derrick never stopped touching her. He explored the hills and valleys of her knuckles, he rested his fingers on her wrist, or traced light, abstract patterns near her elbow.

Anna found his touch enticing and seductive. It wasn't as if he was touching any intimate part of her body—just her hand and arm. But the manner in which he touched her… She found his slow languorous movements very…sensuous…stimulating…arousing.

The white porcelain coffee cups were empty and the sun was sending slanting rays of rosy light through the large, plate-glass window at the front of the shop. Evening diners were converging through the door in small groups. And sometime during the last couple of hours, another waitress had joined the one who had served Anna and Derrick.

"I really should be getting home," she told him. But she knew her tone clearly revealed her unwillingness to leave his company.

"And I'm sure Timmy's wondering where I am."

They looked at each other, yet neither of them made a move to leave. Their waitress had long since dropped off the check, and it sat by Derrick's elbow, a terrible reminder that there was a world outside this quaint little shop, a world that awaited their return.

Finally he scooped up the small, pink check and said, "Well, shall we?"

Anna heaved a sigh. These had been two of the most wonderful hours she'd ever spent in her life.

She let him usher her to the front of the shop, and he only let go of her arm long enough to hand the woman at the register some money. He held the door open for her and they went, side by side, down the sidewalk. And with each step she wished these moments with him could go on.

When they reached his car, Anna was surprised when he continued to propel her forward.

Her glance was questioning.

"Just a few more minutes," he said.

His plea mirrored her own thoughts so exactly that she felt her heart was going to melt right then and there. The magnetism that sparked in the air intensified. If they weren't in such a public place, she just might give in to the overpowering urge she felt to take his hand.

He, too, must have felt the shift in the atmosphere around them, because he released her elbow and slid his hand around her waist. His touch was warm and firm, and the heat of him immediately penetrated her sweater.

They reached the corner of the block and Derrick guided her down the narrow side street.

"Have you ever seen the park at this time of day?" he asked.

Not with you, she wanted to say, but couldn't bring herself to let go completely and actually do it. She simply shook her head from side to side.

"Well," he said, "it's beautiful." He grinned down at her. "And if we're lucky, we may be able to find a little privacy."

A thrill of excitement and anticipation scampered across her skin and she pressed her hand to her abdomen to quell it. *Don't allow this to go too far,* a tiny voice inside her head warned. Having cappuccino in a public coffee shop with him was one thing, but slinking off to locate a private spot in the park was quite another.

Oh, please, her brain pleaded in frantic silence, *just a few more minutes.*

Hearing her mind mimic the very words Derrick had said somehow caused the rational and sensible doubt to fade into the back of her mind, a place far enough away from this dream she was enjoying for her to ignore it altogether. It wasn't very often she allowed herself to indulge in true-life fantasies. She wanted desperately to relish every single second of this one.

This end of the park was lush, secluded and quiet. Faintly, Anna could make out the shouts and cheers from the parents of the children who played baseball at the far corner of the park.

They came upon a weathered, wooden bench that faced a wide, shallow creek. Almost telepathically, the two of them chose this as the spot to sit down. And they spent several quiet minutes enjoying the lazy flow of the water toward the bay.

The sky was turning from a rosy tinge to a dark, violet mauve.

Anna could no longer contain the sigh of contentment that suddenly escaped her lips. "It's exceptionally beautiful," she said, not daring to voice the rest of her thought that what made it *exceptional* was the fact that she was sitting here enjoying the sunset with him.

The weight of his arm fell across her shoulders and she relaxed against it. Why shouldn't she? she wondered, still fighting off a shadow of the doubt she'd been feeling. This is what she wanted.

It's what you want, a stern voice reared up in her head. *But, remember, it's only for the moment!*

"Okay," she muttered in a harsh whisper, banishing for good the silent, cautioning lecturer inside her.

"What's okay?"

The sound of his deep, rich tone poured over her, and she fought off the instant of disconcertion at having been overheard verbally arguing with herself by grinning shyly.

"Nothing," she said softly.

"No," he said. "I want to know."

He touched her chin with firm fingertips and guided her gaze to his. "I really do," he said. "What did you mean? What are you thinking?"

She shrugged one shoulder a fraction. "I was thinking," she began, "that it's okay that I'm here. With you."

That was close enough to the truth for her to be able to give him a tiny smile.

"I'm glad you feel that way," he said.

She heard the inflection in his voice turning deeper, more sensual, and the electricity in the air snapped and skittered around them.

"Are you cold?"

His question made her aware that she'd been totally oblivious to the chilly breeze that had picked up. This was the time of year when the days were still hot and sultry with leftover summer temperatures, but the evenings cooled quickly with the early sunset.

"It's not too bad," she said, but was terribly happy when he pulled her closer, wrapping his other arm around her protectively.

"Is this better?" he murmured huskily.

"Mmmm," she said. "Much."

The only thing that could make this fantasy perfect, she mused, is to feel your lips on mine.

Just as if he'd heard her speak the words aloud, Derrick slowly...sensually...inched forward. And Anna knew without a doubt that her ultimate dream was about to come true.

Chapter Eight

He kissed the corner of her mouth, gently, sweetly, and the timorous reserve he displayed took Anna by complete and utter surprise. She'd thought that his commanding nature would compel him to cover her lips with his in an urgent and frantic manner. That's what she'd been prepared for.

But she was by no means disappointed, for she found this soft beginning achingly erotic.

Slowly he moved to the opposite corner of her mouth, the tender, affectionate touch of his lips so at odds with the timpani she felt thumping behind his rib cage. The pulsing of her own heart throbbed in her ears and at the very tips of her fingers, heightening her senses of hearing and touch.

His next kiss was square on her lips, but it was as light and mild as the whisper of a dove's wing.

Anna felt her palms grow moist, and she had to battle the urge that swept through her to scrunch up his shirt front in her fists and pull him to her. She won the war over the impulse by telling herself to savor each moment as it came. However, the victory didn't lessen the desire that coursed through her veins like liquid fire—to the contrary—the restraint she forced on herself only served to heighten her passion until she thought she would die from wanting to taste him, touch him.

When he trailed a row of tiny, heated kisses to her ear, she turned her head to give him full access. Her eyelids lowered of their own volition, and raw pleasure skittered across the muscles in her neck as his lips teased her skin on one side, his fingertips on the other.

The first sign of his growing bolder was when he nipped her earlobe with his teeth and then automatically soothed the sensuous pain with his hot, silky tongue. He drew her earlobe between his lips, and when he sucked gently, Anna expelled a throaty gasp.

Lifting the weight of her flowing hair, he moved down the length of her neck. His kisses scorched a path downward until the neckline of her sweater barred him from going further.

Derrick lifted his head, and she felt helplessly imprisoned by the heated passion she clearly saw in his glittering gaze. Anna instantly realized that he, too, was bridling the desire he felt. She experienced a sudden flash of fear in the knowledge that, if they were to both allow their emotions to burst free, they would spark a fire so hot and so uncontrollable they would be wholly consumed by the flames that would dance and lick around them in abandon.

He must have read the panic in her eyes, because he inched his face from her in a motion she knew was meant to reassure.

"It's okay." His voice was low and hoarse.

He wanted to calm her, she knew, and the tiny, two-word phrase was a sort of oath—a vow that would let her know she was safe here with him. That nothing would happen that she didn't want to happen.

The smile that gently curled her lips was one of appreciation. She wanted him to know she was not only grateful for his pledge of security, she treasured it like it was worth more to her than precious bars of pure gold.

She was safe. The thought pacified the sudden alarm that had swept through her. But was that what she really wanted? To be safe and secure?

Every fiber of her being screamed a negative assertion.

She searched his gaze in the dwindling daylight and felt the desire inside her become roused and heated until it was simmering just below the surface of self-control.

No, she decided with crystal certainty, she did not want to be safe and secure at this moment. She did not want to be protected from the overwhelming feelings boiling inside her. And even more than that, she wanted desperately to tap into the emotions she could see seething and churning in Derrick.

When she moved her hand, the action was deliberate and unhurried. She took the palm that had been pressed against his chest and now slid it to cup his jaw. She tilted her head, resting it on his biceps.

"Kiss me," she whispered, recklessness and desperation thick in her tone. With her eyes, her thoughts, her posture and only the slightest pressure of her hand, she led him inexorably toward her. "Kiss me, now."

His mouth closed over hers, and Anna felt her world spiral and spin, loop and turn in some fantastic, chaotic ride. But rather than run from the experience, she knew without a doubt that she wanted to strap herself in and enjoy the exciting excursion.

She felt the velvet heat of his tongue whisper across her lips, and every nerve in her body came alive. Her fingers reached up and slid to the back of his head, his short hair tickling her sensitive palm. Needing to feel his bare skin, she maneuvered her other hand into the collar of his dress shirt, and feeling totally risqué, she slid it into the curve between his shoulder and neck. The heat that emanated from him left her breathless.

Inhaling slowly, she strived to hold on to sanity. He smelled of warm, heady spices, and it mingled pleasingly with the aroma of the pine trees all around them. He breathed through his nose, and the sound of it so near her ears was deafening and explicitly carnal.

Her breasts became heavy, her nipples tightening against the soft fabric of her sweater until they were almost painful. She wanted not only to taste him but to feel his hands on her body, but before she could do anything about it, she became distracted as he nibbled her lips open.

The faint taste of cappuccino was on his tongue as it skittered across her teeth. She happily met him and together they deepened the kiss.

Her hand slid to his cheek, and somewhere in the back of her mind she noted that his jaw was the tiniest bit rough with a new growth of whiskers. She found the bristly texture of his skin to be quite sexy and let her fingertips rove lightly.

His touch lowered from her neck, never breaking contact, and came to rest just below her rib cage. His thumb grazed the swell of her breast. She stifled a hungry gasp, and he evidently perceived her reaction, because in an instant the weight of her breast was cupped in his palm.

The intensity and fervor of his kiss increased, and Anna felt herself whirling out of control. The pad of his thumb rubbed across one swollen nipple.

"Oh, God," she groaned in a husky whisper.

The sound of Anna's words sent even more adrenaline racing though his already overloaded system. If he didn't feel her skin against his—right now, this very moment—he would surely go mad.

With great reluctance he released his hold on her breast and let his hand shift around behind her. He slipped his fingers under the waistband of her sweater and slid his flattened palm up the bare skin of her back.

Her flesh was smooth as hot satin, her spine long and gently ridged, and the feel of her drove him wild with wanting. He buried his nose in the flowery fragrance of her thick, dark hair and pulled her tight to his chest.

The small, metal clasp of her bra grated against the fleshy part of his hand. He could feel her heart fluttering like the wings of a hummingbird. His own pulse throbbed and thudded through his body at a rate that must certainly be dangerous to his health. He didn't care.

All he wanted was to be near this woman, to taste her wine red lips, to touch her silken skin, to smell her hot, mysterious fragrance, to hear her call his name in ecstasy. The only sense he'd omitted was that of sight, and although he didn't know it at the moment, it was that very sense that would be his undoing.

He pulled back, shifting the position of his hand on her bare skin, and when he did, her sweater raised just enough for him to see a sliver of her black, lacy bra.

Derrick sat mesmerized for only a split second before dragging his eyes to hers. The desire displayed in her gaze rocked him to the core of his being, and the last shred of control he'd had was ripped away.

His kiss wasn't gentle now, and he tugged at the soft sweater she wore, conscious of the fuzzy fabric between his fingers. He plundered her mouth, and she met and matched his frenzied energy.

She was panting now, he heard it somewhere on the periphery of awareness. And her frantic efforts to unbutton his shirt made his own breathing go ragged.

Then, somewhere in the farthest reaches of his brain, he heard a faint and faraway sound that fought for his attention. A warning. A sign of caution that his subconscious wanted him to heed.

Derrick wanted more than anything in his life to ignore whatever it was that—

Wait! He heard it again.

With great reluctance he dragged his attention from the intimate little circle he and Anna had created. He lifted his head, placing a quelling hand over Anna's fingers as they worked to manipulate another button.

"Wait."

A cheer, his brain reasoned. That's what he'd heard. A distant cheer had risen from the crowd across the way.

He and Anna were in a public park! And here he was trying to get her out of her clothes as though he were some randy, hot-blooded teenager. How could he be so stupid? How could he have let things go so far?

He swallowed hard. "We can't do this here," he said, the words actually paining his raw throat.

"Of course," she murmured.

And it killed him to see her beautiful face color with embarrassment.

"No, no," he said softly, taking her chin in his fingers and forcing her to look at him. "This was my fault."

They bantered back and forth, each taking the blame in whispery voices.

Finally she chuckled, a deep and sexy sound that took him off guard.

"Okay," she said. "It's all your fault." Then she grinned at him. "But I must tell you that I certainly enjoyed myself."

She reached out to refasten the buttons of his shirt, and he held himself very still, taking pleasure from her ministrations.

When she was finished, she smoothed her hand down the front of his shirt. "All better," she said lightly.

The urge to hug her came upon him quickly and abruptly. He stood and held out his hand to her.

"If I don't hold you close," he told her, "I think I'm going to go out of my mind."

"Well, we can't have that, now, can we?"

He found her smile seductive, even though he didn't think she meant for it to be. But the sight of her luscious, still-moist mouth curling so alluringly reignited in him the fierce fire of passion he'd just tried to smother.

The feel of her slender fingers sliding into his palm only served to fan the flame of his desire. He pulled her to her feet and enfolded her in his arms.

He knew she was bound to feel how his body had reacted to her nearness, to her kiss, but he didn't care.

He wanted her to know what she did to him. He wanted her to know how very much he craved her.

She wrapped her arms around him, rested her head on his chest and hugged him tight, and it was like being jolted with a thousand watts of electric current.

He wrestled and then warred with the need and frustration that poured through his body.

"We need to get away from here," he said, irritated by the distress he heard in his own voice.

Hell, he thought, why fight it? You wanted her to know how you feel. Tell the woman how you feel!

"I can't stay here with you." He kept the words as candid as possible, even though they came out a bit ragged. "I just can't be responsible for my actions—"

She placed her warm fingers against his mouth, stopping him from finishing what he wanted to say.

"I understand," she said. "I understand perfectly."

He took her hand, and as they walked back in the direction of his car, he felt...good, and he was having the damnedest time keeping himself from strutting like a rooster.

"I say get rid of her."

The strong, gruff statement was so like Reece that Derrick couldn't help but grin. In fact, he'd anticipated his friend's negative opinion and it didn't even affect Derrick's shot as he eyed up the cue ball and dropped the seven neatly into the corner pocket.

"Great shot," Reece conceded. "But I still say get rid of her. Before things go too far."

Too late. The two little words flashed into Derrick's thoughts, making him chuckle. He didn't dare explain to Reece and Jason just how much Anna had come to mean to him. Hell, how could he tell his friends how he felt, when he couldn't quite put it into words for himself?

"Look, Reece—" Jason crossed his arms over his chest as he stood on the sidelines watching the game "—don't go throwing around advice when you have so little information to go on."

"Oooo," Reece said, chalking the end of his cue stick, "the cop in you is showing there, Jason."

Derrick laughed aloud, his stick glancing off the cue ball and barely rolling it forward an inch.

"That shot counts," Reece called gleefully. "Sorry, buddy. My turn."

"You rat." But Derrick stepped back from the table and gave a slight bow to show his good-natured sportsmanship.

"Hey, if I want to win—" Reece lined up his shot "—then I have to take every advantage."

"You *are* a rat," Jason intoned flatly.

Reece smiled brightly. "The day you guys stop calling me names," he said, "is the day I know our friendship is over." He bent over the billiard table and made another clean shot.

"Let's get back to Anna," Jason said, directing his gaze at Derrick. "You've told us that you've seen her a couple of times. She's helped a lot with Timmy. I say go for it. Who knows? She just may be your—" he searched the ceiling for a second "—soul mate, or whatever the heck they're calling it these days."

"You're a big boy," Reece commented to Jason. "You're allowed to curse. It's okay to say *hell*."

Jason's eyes narrowed. "You know I'm trying to cut out the bad language."

"Gina's not here," Reece pointed out as he glanced

around the nearly empty pool hall. "She can't hear a word you're saying."

"But, Reece, the point is that I want to stop using bad language all together."

"Oh-h-h, so that's the point."

Jason glared. "You are such an ass. How's that for bad language?"

Reece gave a hearty laugh. "Keep calling me names," he said. "It lets me know you care."

"Are you going to play pool?" Derrick asked, his tone long-suffering. "Or are you going to stand here and bicker all night like two old ladies?"

"Don't even dignify that question with an answer, Reece," Jason said, siding with the friend he'd just been quarreling with. "Just take your time...and beat the pants off the man. He needs to learn who's the better pool player."

Reece was quiet a moment as he marked his next shot.

"As I was saying," Jason went on, "Anna might turn out to be the love of your life."

"God help us all," Reece grumbled.

"I'm serious here," Jason said. "Marie was the love of my life. We did everything together." He was quiet a moment. "I still can't believe she's...gone."

Derrick glanced at Jason. Every time the man talked about his deceased wife he grew melancholy and seemed riddled with guilt. Derrick wanted to keep that from happening tonight.

"Since I've met Anna," Derrick said, raising his voice in order to really capture Jason's attention, "I can't think of anything else. The woman is just so...hot." He grinned as he spoke the last word.

He thought that Anna probably wouldn't appreciate

being talked about in such a manner, but he was only doing so to keep Jason from dwelling on the fact that he was a widower.

"Yeah?"

It was Reece whose eyes glittered with curiosity.

"Yeah," Derrick tossed out at Reece absently. "Hey, Jason—" he waved to get his attention "—the other night Anna and I were out together, just taking a walk, and we couldn't seem to keep our hands off each other."

Derrick hated that he was boasting about his conquests, like a great ape pounding on his chest.

"Yeah?"

Again it was Reece who stepped closer, the pool game forgotten.

"You idiot," Derrick hissed at Reece. He jerked his head to get Reece to notice the way Jason was once again gazing off into his own little world, slipping into depression.

"You know," Jason said softly, "I don't remember it being like that between Marie and me." He looked across the table at the two of them. "That fiery passion was never there."

Reece laughed. "That's because you and Marie were an old married couple before you even started," he joked. "You got married way too early."

"Right out of high school," Jason said automatically.

This time Reece's laugh held a bitter edge, and he said, "Well, while Jen and I were married, she was much too busy working on her career to go necking in the woods."

"Anna and I were not necking in the woods," Derrick felt forced to defend his actions. Then he couldn't help but grin as he added, "It was the park."

Both of his friends found his confession extremely funny and insisted on making lewd comments which Derrick chose to ignore. The two of them might be razzing him, he realized, but at least Jason seemed to have snapped out of his somber mood. Derrick thought the weight of guilt Jason carried in regard to his wife's death was overwhelming, but he had no idea how to help his friend. All Derrick felt he could do was be there when Jason needed him—even during those times Jason himself didn't know he was in need.

"So when do you plan on seeing Anna again?"

The question came from Jason, whose brows were lifted high.

One of Derrick's shoulders jerked up in a quick shrug. "I don't know," he admitted.

"The necking in the park was too much for you, hey?" Reece taunted. Then he pointed across the table. "Eight ball in the side pocket."

"No," Derrick said staunchly. "It wasn't too much for me. It's just that she's a little skittish. And I don't want to scare her off."

The eight ball dropped into the side pocket.

"I won!" Reece called out. "Rack 'em up, Jason. The next game's between you and me."

"What makes you think she's skittish?" Jason asked Derrick, as he plunked all the balls into the plastic, triangular-shaped rack.

"Well..." Derrick began, sorry now that he'd brought up the subject, "it's just that she was a little hesitant about seeing me."

He remembered her words and still wondered what

she meant by them. "It wouldn't be a good idea. Trust me."

"She's hiding something," Reece piped up. "You can bet on it."

"Reece," Jason snapped, "how can you say that when you don't know a damned thing about the woman?" Then realizing what he'd said, his face grew scarlet with quick anger. "Damn it, Reece! You made me curse."

"And you did it like a true, red-blooded male." Reece grinned.

"You ass," Jason murmured. He snatched the cue stick from Derrick. "I'm going to win this game if it kills me." He bent over the table and aimed at the neatly arranged balls.

"But she *did* go out with you?" Reece looked pointedly at Derrick, his brows raised.

"Yes, she did."

The cue ball clattered into the others, and all the balls scrambled around on the table, yet none went into a hole.

Jason looked over at Derrick. "And didn't you just finish telling us that when the two of you went out—to the *public* park—you couldn't keep your hands off each other?"

"Yes, I did."

Reece and Jason exchanged keen glances.

"Looks to me," Jason said to Reece, "like our friend here is conjuring problems where none exist."

Reece shrugged. "You know how those analytical types are."

"Exactly," Jason agreed.

Both men turned to Derrick and simultaneously asked, "So when are you seeing her again?"

Derrick actually turned red in the face. He shook his head. "Well, I am planning on going into school next week."

Reece and Jason remained silent, waiting for him to explain further.

"Anna sent a note home with Timmy," he told them. "Apparently she sent one home with all her students. It seems that no one signed up to help in class at the beginning of the school year. She has a project coming up and she needs some help. I plan to volunteer."

Reece groaned. "You're going to be room mother?"

"Room parent," Derrick quickly corrected. "I'm going to be room parent." He pointedly ignored Reece by directing his next statement at Jason. "Anna is also organizing a Career Week. I think it's a great idea. Important enough for me to arrange my schedule so I can go in and tell the kids what it's like to be an accountant in the Navy."

"Oh, my," Reece sniggered, "the exciting life of a military money man."

Derrick laughed despite himself, but that didn't prevent him from tossing a parting shot. "Jason's right. You really are an ass."

"But you do love me," Reece said. "I know you do."

"Anyway," Derrick said. "If I can get her to organize her project the same day I go in for Career Week, then I'll only have to take one day away from the office."

"Sounds as though you have it all figured out," Jason said.

"Just one thing—" Reece waited until both sets of eyes were intently on him "—there won't be much kissy-pooh going on with thirty kids watching your every move."

"There is that," Jason commiserated. "You need to get the woman out on a date. Alone."

"I know," Derrick agreed. "And I plan to do just that when I'm in her classroom next week."

"Geez," Jason exclaimed, "look at the time. I have to be home to tuck Gina into bed in forty minutes."

"Yeah," Reece said, "I need to go over Jeffrey's homework, so I need to go soon, too."

"Me, too," Derrick said.

Jason placed his cue stick on the billiard table. "What do you guys say to grabbing a quick soda before we all have to run home?"

"Sounds good to me," Derrick said.

The three of them started toward the door of the pool hall.

Once they were out on the sidewalk, Reece tapped Jason on the shoulder. "You know you quit the game because you were afraid I'd beat you."

"In your wildest dreams," Jason said.

Derrick only laughed.

Chapter Nine

"Okay, boys and girls—" Anna kept her tone quiet, knowing it was the quickest way to get the attention of all the students in her class "—we need to get our morning routine started. We have a big day ahead of us."

Her calm voice was in direct opposition to the excitement that coiled like a tight spring inside her belly. Derrick was coming into school today.

"Let's stand for the Pledge of Allegiance," she said.

She murmured the memorized words, but her mind was most definitely on other things—primarily Derrick and the feelings he conjured in her.

The man was sexy. She stifled a grin that tugged on one corner of her mouth as she said, "With liberty and justice for all." There was no other way to describe him. There just wasn't.

"Everyone needs to sit down and take out a piece of paper," she said, "so we can write our daily weather report."

Immediately, small hands shot up into the air as children requested to use the pencil sharpener. It was part of the early-morning ritual, and Anna patiently took it in stride. After the Christmas holiday each year, she introduced a new rule that the boys and girls must remember to prepare themselves and their supplies before class actually started. Anna knew this was a normal part of learning responsibility.

As she waited for the line at the sharpener to dwindle, her mind drifted back to Derrick. The emotions that whipped through her body when she was with him were overwhelming. There was something about him that made her feel...gloriously sensual...stunningly beautiful—even though she knew there was nothing special about her looks. It was just that Derrick—

She blinked several times, suddenly cognizant of the utter silence in the room. The children were sitting at their desks, fresh, shiny faces staring expectantly at her. Her cheeks flushed with heat, and she made a silent vow to remain focused on the here and now.

"Who would like to give me a sentence describing the weather this morning?" she asked.

"It's sunny out," Eric said.

Radiantly sunny, she thought. When she'd stepped outside for the first time that morning, she remembered thinking the sunlight was somehow brighter. But that was ridiculous, and she knew it must have something to do with the ebullience bubbling through her at the thought of seeing Derrick.

Forcing herself to concentrate, Anna said, "Can you be a little more descriptive? Can you express what you mean without using the word *it?*"

Eric frowned deeply as he thought. Then his eyes perked up and he tried again, "The sun is shining."

"Very good." Anna turned to the blackboard and wrote the words. Then she pivoted on her heel to face her students again. "Anyone else want to give me a sentence about the weather?"

Amy raised her hand, but remained silent as she waited to be called on.

Anna was surprised. Amy was the shyest child in her class and never volunteered to speak.

"Yes, Amy?"

"The leaves are pretty," the little girl said, her voice whisper quiet.

"Aw, Amy," Billy Davis said. "That don't have nothin' to do with the weather. You're dumb."

"Billy, name-calling is against the rules," Anna calmly chastised. "You know that, and you also know that the punishment for name-calling is missing ten minutes of today's recess."

She directed her gaze at Amy. "Actually, Amy, when the leaves change color, it has a lot to do with the weather. As the days get shorter and cooler, the green chlorophyll growth in the leaves dies and then we are able to see other colors. The plant process of turning sunlight into energy is called photosynthesis, and we'll be learning more about it during science over the next few weeks." Anna smiled at the child. "I like your sentence. And I think it's great that you noticed how beautiful the leaves are becoming." Then she grinned. "They'll soon be as colorful as the paper leaves we've made as an art project."

Anna indicated the multicolored leaf shapes cut from construction paper dangling from the ceiling.

She spoke aloud as she printed the words on the board, "The leaves are turning pretty colors."

"Aw, geez—"

Anna's eyebrows rose as she shot Billy a stern look of warning.

"—but do we gotta say *pretty?*" the boy asked. "That's a sissy word."

A couple of the other boys murmured in accord.

April, the peacemaker, piped up, "How about if we come up with another word that would fit for the boys to use?"

Pandemonium broke out for several seconds as various adjectives were bandied about. Finally the children settled on the word *awesome,* and Anna spelled out the word on the blackboard.

When she was about to ask for a third sentence for the weather report, Anna saw Amy's arm slip timidly into the air.

"Yes, Amy?"

The little girl took a moment to glance down at the floor before she spoke. "Miss Maxwell, I like *awesome* better than *pretty,*" she said. "Can I use *awesome?*"

Anna watched as several other girls in the class bobbed their heads up and down.

Addressing everyone, Anna said, "You may use either word. But class, remember that the weather report is to be written as carefully and neatly as possible. Take your time and do the best you can."

And so the morning went. Reading, arithmetic and story time, all riddled with small, unexpected incidents that only children can create—incidents that kept Anna on her toes and loving her job.

At ten forty-five, Anna had the children take a quick rest room and water fountain break, and then she herded them back into the room for social studies. She'd worked hard contacting and scheduling some of the children's parents to come in for what she called

Career Week. Mr. Styes, the school principal, had been impressed with Anna's idea to have the parents visit the classroom to talk about what they did for a living.

Anna had invited a secretary, a dentist and an auto mechanic to explain to the children what their jobs entailed. The kids whose parents had come in to talk had been very proud. Today, Timmy had bragged several times that Derrick would be coming in. Anna was happy that the time for him to arrive had finally come. No, she had to admit, she was more than happy, she was ecstatic.

She was helping a little boy refasten his belt when a flurry of noise and activity near the door alerted her that Derrick had arrived.

"Okay, everyone," she said to the twittering boys and girls, "let's take our seats so we can welcome our guest."

The children scrambled to their desks, and Anna felt the atmosphere in the room condense with the excitement her students felt—the excitement *she* felt.

She walked toward the door. Or was she slowly sauntering? she wondered, and smiled.

Finally, Derrick's gaze lifted to her face, and Anna felt her physical reality slow to a crawl. His sexy, oh-so-kissable mouth tilted into a charming grin. His dark eyes glinted, clearly expressing to her that he was feeling the same kind of gut-churning excitement as she, and she found the knowledge…highly arousing.

She had to admit to herself that she felt just the slightest bit wicked for feeling titillated with twenty-eight little observers in the room. Striving for natural and normal behavior would be imperative. She grinned inwardly, noting that a little exhilaration would never hurt her—as long as she kept it to herself.

Anna smiled a welcome and offered her hand, just as she had to the secretary, the mechanic and the dentist earlier in the week. "Hello," she said, her eyes riveted to Derrick's face. She was unable to stifle the extra warmth that crept into her greeting, the extra warmth that hadn't been present with the other parents.

His palm slid across hers—the contact warm, sensuous, surprisingly stimulating—and he grasped her hand.

"I'm so glad you could come," she said, the words coming out in a way that made her sound breathless and spent. It was the sight of his handsome face, she told herself, that had her feeling so out of control.

"I'm happy to be here."

The intensity of his gaze sent her a personal message—a message that let her know in no uncertain terms that *she* was the source of his happiness. A shiver coursed across her skin, and she pulled her hand from his before she surrendered to the urge to slip into his arms.

She turned quickly to her class. "Okay, boys and girls." She glanced out over the heads of her students, taking a moment to gather her wits about her. "I'd like to introduce Mr. Derrick Cheney. You all know Timmy. Mr. Cheney is Timmy's godfather. And he's here today to tell us—"

"What's a godfather?"

The enthusiastic query came from the back of the room. Anna stopped for an instant, debating over whether or not to answer the question. Moving from the door to her desk at the front of the room, she decided that the inquiry was sincere and the subject interesting enough to take a moment to explain.

"A godfather is a man who sponsors someone—in

this instance, Timmy—at the time of baptism or christening.''

''What's baptism?'' another child asked.

''I was a baby when I was baptized,'' a little girl said. ''I don't remember it, but my mommy told me all about it and showed me the beautiful dress I wore.''

''My godfather gives me money on my birthday.''

Then several children began to talk at once.

''Okay, quiet,'' she said. ''Remember the rule, one person speaks at a time.''

She glanced over her shoulder at Derrick and smiled apologetically. Although she quickly brought her gaze back to her students, she was struck with the thought that there was something about Derrick's appearance—something that made her want to look his way again. However, she forced herself not to, knowing she had a job to focus on here.

The children quieted, and Anna went on, ''We need to pay close attention to Mr. Cheney now. He's here to talk—''

She'd intended to shoot a quick glance his way as a polite means of including him in the conversation. But her eyes stuck to him like white, tacky glue, and the rest of her sentence was left unsaid as her gaze traveled down his body and she admired his Naval Reserve uniform.

The white, short-sleeved shirt was close fitting, its shoulder boards enhancing Derrick's broad shoulders. The razor-edge crease in the white trousers amplified his already-tall form. His white, round hat had a shiny black visor-type brim and an elaborately embroidered anchor on the front that looked quite dashing sitting atop his head. Standing there, with his arms at his sides, he looked strong, able to conquer even the mightiest of enemies. And she was filled with a sudden pride that he was part of the armed forces bent on protecting the country during times of war.

She had never in her life realized that she had a "thing" for men in uniform. But he looked so sexy, she decided, her gaze riveted to his hat as he removed it and tucked it under his arm.

Dragging her eyes to his face, she could see that he had discerned exactly what she was thinking and feeling. And he was enjoying it!

She nearly gasped aloud when he lowered one eyelid in a quick, yet undeniable, wink.

"I'm an accountant," he said, taking over her speech. "But as you can see from my uniform, I'm also in the Navy. I'm part of the Naval Reserves."

His voice became a drone and Anna felt as if she were in some slow-motion film as she moved behind her desk on shaky legs and sat down.

Never in her life had a man affected her this way. Never, ever. The weakness in her knees, the giddiness in her stomach, the excitement that heightened each of her senses; all of these things made her feel so...so...vibrantly alive.

She only half heard what he told the children, was only half-aware of her students' enjoyment. But on a subconscious level, she knew from the children's easy and animated reaction to him that he was making his complicated occupation understandable and interesting for the six- and seven-year-old boys and girls.

The kids were still asking questions when the yard attendant came to the door to collect the children for recess.

She stood up and rounded her desk. "Children, we

need to thank Mr. Cheney for coming in to visit us,'' she told them.

Everyone sang a chorus of thank-yous before rushing toward the door.

"Wait," Anna called. "I need you to come directly into class from recess. No dawdling. Because we're going to be making homemade pizza for our lunch."

The children shouted their glee.

"And Mr. Cheney has agreed to stay and help us."

There was another flurry of activity as the children filed out the door.

"Oh, Billy," Anna said.

The boy looked at her.

"Remember your ten-minute punishment."

"Aw," he said, scrunching up his face distastefully.

The yard attendant nodded at Anna and took Billy in hand.

Timmy was the last to approach the door, and before exiting, the child stopped and turned to Derrick. "Thanks," he said, his little face beaming with pleasure.

Derrick grinned down at him. "You're welcome, pal," he said. And then he took off his hat and placed it on Timmy's head.

"I can wear it outside?" Timmy asked.

"Sure," Derrick told him. "Just be careful."

"Great! See ya after recess!" And Timmy disappeared down the hallway with the others.

"You know," Anna said when the room was silent, "thanks to you and that hat, Timmy will be king of the playground today."

"I hope so," he said. "That's why I came." Then his dark gaze intensified and his voice lowered as he added, "Well, one of the reasons, anyway."

His smile turned her knees all mushy again, and reaching out as nonchalantly as possible, she pressed her palm against the desktop for support.

"You...ah," she stammered, suddenly nervous as a schoolgirl, "you were great with the kids."

He chuckled, a rich sound that vibrated from deep in his chest. "And how would you know?" he asked.

Anna did her best to look affronted. "What do you mean?"

Again he laughed. "Every time I looked at you, you were gazing off into space—" he hesitated only long enough for exactly the right shock effect "—or studying my tush."

She nearly choked. "I was not!" she blatantly lied.

They stared at each other for several long seconds, his eyes glittering with a teasing light, hers horrified that he'd seen right through her all along.

Finally she decided it was futile to fib, and she pursed her lips, letting her eyes travel down the long, muscular length of him. Bringing her gaze back up to his face, she said, "Although, if I was going to be entirely truthful, I'd have to tell you that your tush *is* worth studying."

His mahogany eyes darkened with something mysterious. No, she realized. Mysterious described the baffling, the unknown. However, she knew without a shadow of a doubt what was displayed in his gaze.

Desire. Desire for *her*.

"I'm glad you think so."

His tone was thick and husky, and it raised the tiny hairs on the back of her neck.

He stepped toward her, sliding his palms up along her arms and over her shoulders. Gently, caressingly, he framed her face in his hands.

Anna could smell him, the scent of heated soap and spices. His lips pressed against hers in a kiss that was agonizingly sweet and soft.

She moaned, low and muted, for his ears alone.

"It's so good to see you," she whispered. "But..." She let the word trail and allowed her eyes to convey her message by darting to the open doorway and then back to his face.

"I know," he said, inching back away from her. "This isn't the place. But I need you to know how much I—"

Almost in a panic, Anna pressed her fingers to his lips. "I know," she told him in a rush.

Swallowing stiffly, she fought the overwhelming alarm that flared up inside her. She knew exactly what he was feeling, because she was feeling it, too. But for some reason she couldn't bring herself to allow the words to be said aloud.

She pulled her top lip between her teeth as she searched frantically for some way to conquer the wave of panic that had blindsided her.

"Are you okay?" he asked softly.

"Mmm-hmm," she said. "I'm fine." But her voice was squeaky with nerves. What is wrong with me? she wondered.

Her gaze lowered and she found herself staring at the perfectly straight creases that ran down the length of his legs.

"You're not planning on helping to make pizza dough in your uniform, are you?" she asked, desperate to turn the topic to some safer, more neutral ground.

"Oh, no," he assured her. "I brought some civvies...ah, civilian clothes." He chuckled and clarified further by saying, "Casual clothes. They're in that bag." He indicated a zippered gym bag he'd left by the door.

"Good," she said, knowing that focusing on the mundane, the normalcy of her job, was helping her to overcome whatever it had been that had just flashed through her a moment ago. "Because I suspect we'll have flour flying every which way when the kids get back from recess."

"In fact," he said, backing away from her even further, "why don't I find the little boys' room and change my clothes."

It was so obvious to Anna that her sudden change in behavior had him confused. She thought it was best that they separate, if only for a few moments, so she could get herself together.

"I'll be happy to show you—" She stopped, a better idea coming to her. "Why don't you use the adult rest room that's right off the teachers' lounge? You'll be more comfortable there." She forced a smile. "The facilities are normal-size, and you won't have to worry about being intruded upon. Come on, I'll show you."

The heels of her shoes clicked hollowly on the tile floor of the hallway. She paused at the door of the teachers' lounge.

"Here you go," she said. "I have to make a quick trip to the cafeteria for some supplies. I'll meet you back at the room."

"Okay."

As she walked away, she couldn't get the image of his frowning face from her mind. She enjoyed being with him so very much. He made her feel so...wonderful. Inside and out. He wanted her. It was so obvious. But—

The manager of the school cafeteria met Anna at the

door, keeping her from contemplating her thoughts further. Hetta was a woman who loved to cook and loved to eat. She enjoyed planning nutritious meals for the children just as much as she enjoyed making the huge amounts of food necessary to feed all the students who bought hot lunch every day.

Hetta helped Anna load a large, wheeled cart with big, stainless steel mixing bowls, glass measuring cups and spoons for mixing. Then they loaded another cart with flour, a jug of water, yeast, pizza sauce, cheese, pepperoni and various julienne vegetables.

"I'll have the ovens heated and ready for you when you need them," Hetta told her.

"Thanks," she said.

Anna pushed one cart in front of her and pulled the other behind, as she slowly and carefully made her way back to her classroom.

"Here, here," Derrick called, jogging down the hall to catch up with her. "Let me help you."

She smiled her thanks, and was relieved to find that the air was free of the thick anxiety and panic she'd felt a few minutes ago. Putting a little space between them had obviously been a good idea.

She allowed him to take one of the carts, and they maneuvered them one at a time through the doorway and into her classroom.

"I really can't thank you enough for coming in to help me," she told him as she unloaded the mixing bowls and other cooking utensils and placed them on the worktable at the back of the room. "It's getting harder and harder to find a room mother. Room *parent*," she quickly amended along with a smile of apology.

Derrick grinned. "A couple of my friends gave me

a hard time about the title." He, too, began to unload his cart onto the worktable.

"With the way the economy is these days," Anna went on with her small talk, "it's almost necessary for both mothers and fathers to work in order to make ends meet. But that makes it tough for teachers who need volunteer help in the classroom."

"I can understand the problem," he said. "But do you really believe the economy is to blame?"

Anna was quiet a moment as she contemplated his question. "Well, I do know that kids today have more 'things' than in the past. And everything seems to have a name brand on it, which makes shoes, clothes, sneakers—whatever—more expensive." She paused. "I don't know if all that is necessary, but it seems to be what the children want. And it's only natural that their parents want to give it to them."

She bent down to retrieve the large mixing spoons on the second shelf of her cart. "In a perfect world," she said softly, "I'm sure there would be fewer things to buy and more time to spend with loved ones."

The spoons rattled as she placed them on the table. "On the other hand—" she glanced over at him "—I wouldn't want someone to tell me I had to stop working toward a career simply because I'm a woman and I choose to have children."

"I'm not touching that can of worms with a ten-foot pole," he said.

They chatted on, and Anna realized sometime during their conversation that they had once again found that easy rapport they had shared the afternoon he'd taken her for coffee—and the evening he'd taken her to the park.

The children clamored into the room with cacophonous noise and confusion.

"Guard the worktable with your life," she said to Derrick. "Don't let anyone touch anything. I need to make sure everyone washes up,"

"Aye, aye, Captain."

Anna couldn't stop the smile that took over her lips at the sight of his small, sharp salute. She would have liked to share the moment with him, but duty called.

"Okay, everyone," she called. "Let's line up and wash our hands at the sink. Use soap. Scrub those hands really well, and then please put on your art smocks. We don't want to go home with pizza sauce stains on our clothes."

Standing sentinel over the children as they cleaned their hands, Anna glanced toward the back of the room where Derrick was. A few of the kids had washed up, were into their smocks and were drawn to the worktable like slivers of iron to a horseshoe-shaped magnet.

She grinned, admiring the job he was doing keeping her students back from the table. Derrick patiently answered the kazillion-and-one questions she knew her students could easily come up with. He was definitely holding his own.

When the last child had tossed his paper towel into the wastepaper basket, Anna joined Derrick and the rest of the boys and girls at the back of the room.

"Okay," she said, "let's make pizza dough!" She reached for the bag of flour. "We need people for measuring, people for dumping, people for mixing." She glanced at Derrick. "When you have so many children and so few jobs, you learn to break everything down so everyone gets to have a job." She smiled at the sea of faces. "And everyone *does* want to help, right?"

"Yes!" came the resounding reply.

"Mr. Cheney, if you could make one large batch of dough at your end of the table," she said, "and I make one here, we should have enough to go around."

She handed him a recipe she'd found called Pizza for a Crowd.

"I'll dissolve the yeast in water," she told them. "The temperature of the liquid is very important. If the water's too hot, it will kill the yeast. Too cold and it will stunt its growth."

April looked up at her teacher. "What is yeast?"

"Is it alive?" another student asked.

"It looks like sand," Timmy said. Then he laughed. "Miss Maxwell's puttin' sand in our pizza!"

Some of the children hooted, others expressed a strong distaste for the idea.

"All right, settle down," Anna said. "Actually, April, yeast is—"

"May I, Miss Maxwell?"

Anna's brows rose as she caught Derrick's eye. He seemed terribly anxious to join in on the conversation, and she couldn't have been more pleased.

"By all means, Mr. Cheney," she said. "Go ahead."

"Yeast is a living plant," he told the children. "When it's fed with some warm water and a little sweetener, such as sugar or honey, then it gives off a gas that makes the dough rise."

"It gives off gas?" Timmy asked, obviously intrigued by the idea.

"Yeah," Andrew piped up, laughing, "just like my grandfather does when he comes to visit." Then as an aside he added, "My mom hates it when he passes gas."

"Andrew," Anna warned with enough sternness to stop the snickers of the other boys and girls, "another rude comment like that, and you'll be in time-out."

Derrick went on to explain about the gluten in the flour, and Anna was simply amazed at how easily he related cooking to actual science. It was exactly what she wanted her students to learn from this project.

When the dough was mixed, they set it aside to rise while they washed and prepared the vegetables. Finally the adults gave the children small pieces which they could knead and finally flatten into rounds that they would top with sauce, cheese and vegetables or meat.

"Make certain that you use veggie strips or meat strips to form your initials in your pizza," Anna instructed her students. "Otherwise, we won't be able to tell which pizza belongs to you."

While the kids busied themselves topping their pizza dough, Anna and Derrick took this opportunity to wash their hands at the sink.

"I have to tell you," she whispered, "I'm very impressed by how much you know about cooking."

"Well, I have to admit that I didn't know much about it until recently," he confessed. "When I had to start cooking meals for Timmy, I went about learning how, thoroughly and very…systematically."

Anna grinned. "You're an analytical type," she said. "Just like Timmy. Did you notice how interested he was in how yeast works? He likes to *systematically* discover how things work, too. Just like you. You and Timmy have a lot in common."

Derrick glanced over at his godson. "You know, I think you're right."

The tone in his voice told Anna that he hadn't realized it before.

She dried her hands, tossed the paper towel and then offered one to Derrick. He accepted it, but she didn't release it immediately.

His dark gaze met hers, and she felt an odd cessation of time. A raw hunger curled deep in her belly, and she fought the urge to reach out and caress his cheek.

This man, from their very first meeting, had caused her emotions to run riot. From sheer and terrifying panic, to bold and desperate desire and a thousand emotions in between, Derrick made her feel with a depth she'd never before experienced.

"Thanks," she said, knowing that the one tiny word she'd meant to use to show her gratitude for his help today was evincing so much more.

"Believe me—" his voice was rusty with feeling "—I've enjoyed myself today with you and the kids."

Mesmerized by his gorgeous, dark eyes, Anna didn't release her hold on the paper towel until her concentration was intruded upon by one of her students.

"I'm all done," April said.

"Me, too," Billy shouted. "Can we draw on the blackboard?"

"Sure," Anna told them, striving to recover from this heavy, trancelike feeling that had enveloped her. "Just until the others are finished."

Billy scrambled to the board and grabbed the largest piece of chalk. April quickly followed.

Anna focused her attention on Derrick. She felt somehow deprived as he walked away from her, taking a moment with each child to admire his or her pizza creation.

She liked feeling swallowed up by the thick blanket

of wanting and desire he created when he was near her. She liked the way he made her feel…attractive.

Derrick laughed with a little girl, and Anna heard him assure her that her lunch would be delicious. Then he bent over where Timmy was concentrating on spelling his initials with slivers of green pepper. Derrick was so good with the child, so good with all of the children. Fate had done a wonderful thing in making him Timmy's guardian. Derrick was an excellent father figure for Timmy—for any child. In fact, she wouldn't be surprised if Timmy didn't eventually think of Derrick as his real father. Because he certainly would make a wonderful daddy.

Anna blinked, and then her eyes opened wide as the thought jelled and solidified in her mind. Derrick *would* make a wonderful daddy. Hadn't she thought that from the very beginning? Hadn't she come to that conclusion after finding out all the changes in his life he was willing to make—just for Timmy?

She turned to face the wall, confusion and panic churning in her mind at a frantic pace.

Derrick would make a wonderful daddy. The idea reverberated in her mind. Hadn't that been the very reason she'd meant to keep their relationship strictly professional?

The question struck her like a physical blow.

How had this happened? More to the point, why had she allowed it to happen?

"I'm tellin' on you."

Anna turned at the sound of April's voice.

"Miss Maxwell!" the little girl called. "Billy's drawin' pictures of you and Mr. Cheney."

Her gaze darting to the blackboard, Anna saw the two stick figures that Billy had outlined. The scribbled ball connecting the two figures was the child's obvious attempt to show a clasping of hands. Around the entire image, Billy had drawn a huge, lopsided heart.

"Billy," Anna call sharply, "erase that picture this instant."

She heard the near hysteria in her voice. The urge to deliver swift and stern punishment welled up in her. She felt angry and embarrassed, and she heard the majority of her students laughing and jeering at Billy's picture.

But she knew if she were to overreact, her behavior would be more telling to her class than if she were to keep her cool. The boys and girls she taught were young, but they were far from stupid.

She took a deep, cleansing breath. Not daring to look at Derrick, she kept her tone calm as she said to Billy, "Why don't you help Mr. Cheney load the pizzas onto the cart. Then you, Timmy and Mr. Cheney can take them to the cafeteria."

It didn't take the children long to place their pizzas onto the two carts. Timmy and Billy pushed one cart, while Derrick pushed the other out of the classroom and down the hall.

Anna got the other children to help her clean up while they waited for their lunch to cook. Her hands were literally shaking as she lifted a spoon that was dusted with flour.

Dear Lord, she thought miserably. She had let her relationship with Derrick go too far. It hadn't been something she'd meant to do. She remembered hearing—even heeding—her warning signals when she'd first met him. But she'd wanted him so badly that, somewhere down the line, she'd chosen to ignore her internal alarms.

She *had* to make a clean break from Derrick. That was crystal clear in her mind.

But how could she do it without telling him the truth? How could she stop seeing him without utterly humiliating herself?

Chapter Ten

The classroom was a disaster area. From her desk, Anna surveyed the damage. Sure, the children had tried to clean up after themselves, but there were wadded napkins on the floor and several crumpled paper cups that had been missed. She saw bits of leftover pizza crust on the back worktable, and the drips of sticky soda here and there on the floor indicated that she'd have to borrow a mop from the school custodian.

She couldn't believe she'd allowed her students to leave the room in this condition. The fact that she had let them go to their physical education class, leaving the room in such a mess, was confirmation of just how upset and preoccupied she was regarding what she knew she had to do.

"Those kids are great."

Derrick. The sound of his name echoing in her head made her feel terribly sad. Yet at the same time the anxiety roiling inside her had her nerves on edge. She looked over at him.

She had to tell him she couldn't see him anymore. She had to do it today. Right now.

"Hey, are you awake over there?" he asked, his tone silky soft.

He'd been leaning on the doorjamb, looking at her, she guessed. The children had just left, and she could hear the gym teacher shushing them as they went down the hall.

"Yes," she answered. "I heard what you said. And you were great with the kids."

He smiled, and she felt her heart twist painfully.

She didn't want to do this. He'd made her feel like no other man had. But she simply couldn't let it go on. Not for another minute.

"We need to talk," she said.

Derrick came toward her. "I hope you're planning on telling me what's wrong."

"What?" Her eyes widened.

"You don't think I noticed?" he asked. "You don't think I could tell something happened? That you shut yourself off from me somewhere during the pizza-making process?"

His questions were asked in a light, almost breezy manner. It was as though he sensed the heavy cloak of depression that hovered over them and he wanted to lighten it. He'd meant for her to laugh. But the sorrow inside her mingled with apprehension, creating an emotion too overwhelming to allow laughter or jokes. He stopped in front of her desk, and she looked up at him, her gaze as steady as her jittery nerves would allow.

"I can't see you anymore."

There, she thought, it's out in the open. I've said it. He knows. My voice may have been as tight and twangy as an overstretched guitar string, but at least the statement has been made.

His entire demeanor changed right before her eyes; his shoulders squared, his chin tipped upward, the muscle at the back of his jaw ticked as he clenched his teeth. His body language shouted aggression.

"Why?"

She got up, rounded her desk and made her way down one aisle of neatly arranged desks.

"I told you at the very beginning that this wasn't a good idea," she said. She bent down and snatched a balled-up napkin from where it lay on the floor under a chair.

"I know you did," he said. "But I thought we had gotten over that."

She turned to face him. "No, Derrick. I didn't get over it." Then her voice softened. "You just…blinded me for a while."

"What do you mean?"

His tone was sharp and louder than Anna would have liked. She hurried to the door and closed it so they couldn't be overheard.

"Look," she said, keeping lots of distance between them. It was easy to do since he hadn't moved an inch from her desk. "I don't want to fight. I don't even want to argue. I just need you to know that I…I can't see you anymore."

He was silent, and Anna went down another aisle, absently picking up two cups that had been kicked aside. Moving toward the back of the room, she tossed the cups and the napkin into the wastebasket.

Facing him was something she couldn't seem to do, so she busied herself at the worktable wiping up bits of green pepper and cheese with a large sponge.

"Anna."

His hands on her shoulders made her jump, and she gasped as he said her name.

"It's true that I've only known you for a few weeks..."

She was relieved that he didn't move to turn her around. She grabbed the table edge for emotional support, clenching the sponge in one tight fist. If she wasn't careful, Derrick would cause her to lose herself in the chaotic feelings that churned inside her stomach.

"But I've come to realize that you're an intelligent woman. You know that there's something between us. Something special. I recognized it from the very beginning. And I know you did, too."

Hot tears burned behind her eyelids. She wouldn't cry. She wouldn't! She had to get through the rest of the day. The rest of her life.

Please don't do this to me, she silently begged. Please don't make me tell you things that will make you hate me.

She strained against the pressure of his hands as he turned her to face him, but finally she had to surrender. Her lids felt as though they weighed a thousand pounds as she raised her eyes to meet his.

"We have something special," he said, almost as a proclamation. "Something that doesn't come along between two people very often. We'd be fools to let it go." His whole face softened. "Wouldn't we?"

Lie, her brain frantically ordered. *Tell him he means nothing to you. Tell him you feel nothing.*

A sudden anger sparked in his eyes. "Don't you dare deny that everything I've said is the truth." He glared, his fury raging. "I'm not some moron—"

"Okay, okay," she whispered. She hated the rage she saw in his face. "I'm not denying anything."

Her words seemed to make him relax, but only a little. The energy wavering in the room was still volatile, like silent, pulsing heat lightning just waiting to unleash its pent-up power.

"But," she said, "that doesn't change the fact that I can't see you anymore."

His head tilted a fraction to one side. "Haven't you heard anything I've said?"

"I've heard everything you said," she assured him.

"Then you don't agree with me," he said. "You don't think that whatever is between us is special." He laughed harshly. "Our time in the park was just a cheap thrill for you. It meant nothing."

Now it was her turn to be swept away by an all-consuming anger. "Of course it did! It meant everything!"

The two short sentences had come out in a vicious, unstoppable stream. She hadn't meant to say them, but Derrick, and the fury he'd stirred in her, had forced the words from the very depths of her soul.

"Then why, Anna? Why?"

"Just because!" She broke away from him and took a step back. The sponge she clutched fell to the floor, forgotten.

She crossed her arms over her chest protectively. She wanted badly to run away from him. To run away from the situation. The very last thing she wanted was to look at him, because she knew what she would see in his strong, handsome face. But she was like a moth, he, a flame, and her gaze was drawn to him literally against her will.

His forehead was creased with confusion and hurt—

emotions that *she* was inflicting. He didn't understand the motivation behind her actions, and the bewilderment she left him with was wounding him terribly.

She didn't mean to hurt him. She'd never intended for him to suffer from knowing her. All she'd meant to do was protect herself.

Anna couldn't stand the thought of causing Derrick pain of any kind. And she knew she could easily ease the torment she read in his eyes. By making him understand.

The only way she could do that, she realized, was to be completely and totally honest with him. And that meant opening herself up, making herself vulnerable to the anguish and humiliation she knew in her heart he would feel when he discovered the truth.

But she finally decided Derrick was worth it.

"You made me feel…wonderful," she began, her words halting and difficult, grating with thick emotion. "Too wonderful." Then the sentences seemed to pour from her. "We got too close. Much too fast. You made me feel things I shouldn't feel. You became too important. You came to mean too much."

He shook his head slowly. "Maybe I'm thick or something, but I think those are perfect reasons for us to be together. We *did* get close. But, too close? I don't think so." He moved a step toward her. "And, Anna, you made me feel things, too. Wonderful things." He reached out to her. "I think I may be falling in love with you, Anna."

"Oh, dear God," she said, backing away. "Don't say that!"

There was a rushing wave of sound in her ears, as though a freight train was coming right at her. She felt like sanity was slipping away, and she scraped and

clawed at it, holding tight with the tips of her finger-
nails.

"What is it, Anna? What's the matter?"

She felt his hand on her arm. "No," she snapped,
jerking from him.

Her eyes were wide open, her hands clenched into
tight fists, as she realized that she, too, was falling in
love. Deeply in love. Suddenly the desks, chairs, cab-
inets, the whole classroom, seemed to take on a surreal,
almost cartoonish, feel.

"Can't you see," she blurted, tears springing to her
eyes. "I never meant for us to fall in love. I *knew* that
we shouldn't go out. I *knew* that there was something
about you...something I should stay away from. But I
didn't listen to my protective instincts. I let this happen.
I allowed myself to be swept away. I didn't think. I
didn't *want* to think."

She was losing her mind. She'd lost her mind!

"I enjoyed being with you so very much. I didn't
want to think about ending it. Even though I knew I
would have to." She looked at him, knowing full well
that the madness she was feeling was clearly showing
in her eyes. "And then I saw you here today. With the
children. You're wonderful with Timmy. You're going
to do such a great job of raising him."

Tears scalded a path down her cheeks, and she let
them fall unheeded as she whispered, "You'll make a
wonderful father, Derrick. A wonderful father."

Her throat hurt too badly to say anything else. He
had to understand now. He simply had to.

However, it didn't take her long to realize that he
didn't.

"I hope I can be a good father figure for Timmy,"

he said, clearly baffled by all that she'd said. "But why should that matter—"

"I didn't say father *figure*," she snapped, her frustration showing. "I said *father*. You'll make a wonderful *father*."

He studied her for one silent, intense moment.

Finally he lifted his hands into the air, palms up. "I'm sorry, Anna. I know you're trying to say something important here. But I'm lost."

She raked shaking fingers through her already tousled hair. Her insides were dull and lifeless. The nervousness and agitation she'd felt just moments before seemed to have seeped from her, leaving behind an empty shell.

"I'll never be a mother." Her voice held a flat, monotone sound.

"Of course you will," he quickly assured her. "You'll make a great mom."

"You're not listening," she said, her voice sharp with frustration. "I'll never be a mother, Derrick, because I can't have children. If we were to stay together, I couldn't give you children. And if there's one thing I've learned today—" A sob escaped from her throat—a sob that shocked and astonished her because she'd felt certain there was no emotion—nothing—left inside her. "—it's that you *should* have children," she finished.

A tidal wave of pure, unadulterated panic swept over her. If she saw scorn and rejection on this man's face, it would kill her. In a last desperate act of self-preservation, Anna ran to the front of the classroom, flung open the door and ran away from Derrick, doing her best to choke back her tears with every step.

* * *

The breeze blowing across the bay held the chill of true autumn. Derrick had hoped that taking the boat out for a short sail would help to clear his mind. But it seemed that chaos was determined to reign supreme.

He'd told Anna that he was falling in love with her. He'd had no idea whatsoever that he was going to say such a thing when he'd gone into school earlier today. But when she'd ambushed him like she had, announcing that she didn't want to see him anymore, he'd felt backed into a corner with no way out. His declaration of love had been a secret weapon he hadn't even known he'd possessed. Until the sentence was out of his mouth.

After he'd said the words, however, he'd felt glad about it. Glad that Anna knew his true feelings.

He thought back on it, realizing that Anna had been as surprised by his intimate profession as he had been. More so, in fact. He wanted to close his eyes, but that wouldn't block out the image of the anguish his loving disclosure had caused her. It had ripped him apart inside to see her suffering through an obvious onslaught of emotion all because of something he'd said.

He hadn't understood what was happening at the time. At first, he'd thought that she'd felt the idea of his loving her was horrifying. The way she was carrying on so, continuing to insist that she couldn't see him anymore.

But her behavior hadn't been because she thought his love for her was something bad, something she didn't want. Her words and the emotional upheaval she was experiencing were due to the fact that their relationship had gone farther than she'd intended. She'd gotten too close to him without revealing the secret she kept hidden deep inside. The fact that she couldn't have children.

No! He literally turned his head from the notion, unable just yet to bring himself to think about it.

There was something that Anna had said, though, that had actually given him a pleasant jolt. He smiled as he remembered the roundabout way in which she'd proclaimed her own feelings for him.

I never meant for us to fall in love.

She hadn't said that she'd never meant for him to fall in love with her. No. She used the word *us*. Us— meaning her as well as him.

What Anna had told him was that she, too, had fallen in love. Fallen in love with him.

The idea made him grin like an idiot!

But the afternoon had come to such an awful end. Derrick didn't have to concentrate hard to bring up a mental picture of how Anna had looked just seconds before she'd bolted out the door. Her eyes had been wide, and they had held a wild, frantic, almost captured look. She'd fought the tears, fought them hard, but he'd seen them just the same. The soft, peachy skin that normally covered her face had been pale and taut, and at times, even tortured.

Derrick had wanted to snatch her to him, to hold her close and calm her fears. But she would never have allowed that. Anna was too strong a woman to lean on any man. Yet he felt he could have comforted her, if only she would have let him.

Suddenly, helplessly, he found his thoughts turning to kids.

Before Timmy had come into his life, he hadn't given children much thought at all. But his godson had changed that. He certainly had. Timmy had shown him life from a brand-new perspective. The boy depended on him, and that had made Derrick feel capable and responsible in a way that no "job" ever could. The love he felt for Timmy swelled his heart near to bursting. Even after having the child in his life such a short amount of time, Derrick couldn't imagine life any other way. He couldn't conceive of going back to his solitary life-style. Timmy was a part of his existence, a part of *him,* and he loved the boy dearly. Nothing on heaven or earth could further deepen his feelings for the boy— not even if, by some fantastic miracle, he could become Timmy's real father.

He thought of the other members of The Club. Jason had Gina, and Reece had Jeffrey. The two men had kids of their own. Kids that they had fathered. With women they'd loved. Derrick wondered what that would be like. To share something so very intimate, so very beautiful, with that one someone in the world who meant everything to you.

Derrick tried to imagine himself with a wife—a pregnant wife. What would it feel like to slide his palm over her swelled belly? How would he react to feeling his son or daughter kick for the first time? What would it be like to experience the miracle of birth?

From what he'd discovered today, the woman he loved couldn't give him those experiences. Anna couldn't have children. This was the first time since leaving the school that he'd been able to mentally voice the words.

Heaving a deep sigh, he tacked the boat across the bay and steered toward home.

His analytical brain whispered to him that Anna couldn't give him everything he wanted in a partner.

But his heart told him that he wanted to spend the rest of his life with her.

Another miserable sigh rumbled up from deep in his chest. What the hell was he going to do? And after thinking back on how adamant Anna had been about not seeing him, he couldn't help wondering if there was anything he *could* do.

He tied the boat securely to the mooring and eased over the side into the dinghy. As he rowed toward shore, Derrick felt more alone than at any other time in his life.

He pulled the small rowboat until most of its hull was out of the water. When he turned, he saw Timmy sitting on the back porch.

The boy waved at him, and Derrick waved back as he made his way up the grassy incline toward the house.

"Is Chrissy inside?" he asked as he stepped up onto the deck.

"Yeah," Timmy said. "She's on the phone."

"Oh."

The news didn't really bother Derrick. Chrissy was always good about keeping a close eye on Timmy, so he didn't mind if she talked to her friends on the telephone for a few minutes.

"Can I ask you somethin'?"

"Sure, pal," Derrick said, sitting down next to Timmy on the wooden chaise. "What is it?"

"Well," the boy began, "I been wonderin' about something." He looked up at Derrick. "All of my friends…" He paused, then started again. "Well, most of my friends are always talkin' about their dads. How their dads go places with 'em, and do stuff with 'em. And…well…I was wonderin' if maybe…"

Derrick had to smile at the hard time Timmy seemed to be having at communicating what it was he wanted. Finally he thought it might be nice if he helped the boy out.

"You have someplace you want us to go?" Derrick asked. "Something you want us to do?" He patted Timmy on the leg. "Just say the word, pal, and it's done. Whatever you want."

"Well, that'd be great and all…but that wasn't what I meant."

"Oh," Derrick said. And when Timmy didn't respond right away, Derrick went on, "Come on, Tim. You can talk to me about anything. What's on your mind?"

"I was wonderin' if maybe—" the child looked up at him with vulnerable, almost pleading eyes "—maybe I could call you Dad."

Derrick was absolutely stunned. He didn't know what to say. The request had come at him like a lightning bolt from a clear, sunny sky. Timmy wanted to call him *Dad*.

With his heart twisting painfully and lovingly in his chest, Derrick blinked several times to clear the moisture from his eyes. He was so glad that the sun was setting and the deck was shrouded in shadow.

Then sudden thoughts of his cousin James popped into his head. Timmy's real father had a right to be remembered, and Derrick didn't want to do anything that might diminish the child's memories of James.

"Tim, you know…you had a great dad." Then he realized that bringing James into the conversation might make Timmy feel guilty. "What I mean is…well…" He fumbled for words. Finally he leaned his elbows on his knees and looked at his godson. "Would it bother you?" he asked. "Calling me Dad?"

"Gee, no," Timmy said, shrugging nonchalantly. "It's not like I called my father Dad, or anything."

Derrick couldn't stop the frown that creased his brow. "You didn't?"

Timmy shook his head.

"Well—" his words came slowly because he was hesitant to ask this question "—what did you call him?"

The boy shrugged again. "Sir," he said. "I called him Sir."

A lump the size of a huge rock lodged itself in Derrick's throat. What kind of father-son relationship had Timmy shared with James? Derrick wondered. How could it have been close or loving with such a formal—

Derrick stopped the thought. He couldn't worry about that right now. At this moment he needed to direct all his energy and compassion to this little boy. Then suddenly, emotion overwhelmed him as he realized just what it was Tim was asking. Joy and happiness flooded through him as he thought of this child calling him Dad.

"Well, Tim…" He coughed into his closed fist and then tried again. "Tim, I think it would be great."

"Awesome!" Timmy slid down from the chair and hurried to the sliding glass door. "I can't wait to tell Eric." Then he turned back to Derrick and grinned. "That is if I can ever get Chrissy off the phone."

Derrick chuckled as he watched Timmy slide the door shut. He sat there in the dusky light and let the love he felt for the little boy warm every muscle in his body. He couldn't possibly love Timmy more if the boy were his own child.

Realizing that this wasn't the first time this afternoon that he'd thought those very words, he leaned back against the chaise and stared out at the dark, shining bay.

The love he felt for Timmy was immeasurable. It mattered not one wit that the child was his godson and not his son.

If he could feel such strong emotions for Timmy, why couldn't he feel those same strong emotions for other children—other *adopted* children.

Anna had said that he'd make a wonderful father. And, damn it, she'd make a wonderful mother. The fact that she couldn't have children of her own shouldn't keep her from becoming a mother.

His heart flipped in his chest as realization struck— he *could* spend the rest of his life with Anna, and they *could* have children together.

Granted, they would be somebody else's children, but the love he and Anna would bestow on them would quickly make them theirs. He felt so light, he thought he just might fly. The answer was so easy, he wondered why it had taken him hours to see it.

But then, he realized, he'd probably never have seen the answer if it hadn't been for his discussion with Timmy. God, how he loved that kid!

Okay, he thought to himself, so he saw the answer to his and Anna's problem. Now the question was, how could he go about ripping off her blinders so that she could see it, too?

Anna hefted the strap of her canvas pack farther up on her shoulder. She was certain she'd remembered everything she needed for the day, because last night she'd lost herself—or she'd tried to lose herself—in making the detailed list of supplies.

The elaborate list had been a futile attempt to keep thoughts of Derrick at bay.

She swallowed hard. Just thinking his name caused the sadness and sense of loss to lump in her throat in a firm, tight knot. She shoved him from her thoughts. Doing so was the only way for her to survive.

Reaching out for the large, metal door latch, Anna froze. There, standing in the wide vestibule, was Derrick. She saw him through the thick glass. He was talking with the principal.

An emotional vise clamped around her heart, squeezing and squeezing, until she thought she heard herself moan. The sight of him was wonderful, but that wasn't what caused her reaction. It was the fact that their breakup hadn't affected Derrick in the least. If it had, how could he converse with Mr. Styes with such animation, such vivacity?

Derrick was smiling, waving his arms to make some point. He stuffed one fist into his well-cut dress trousers and chuckled, his shoulders jumping as he laughed. The sight of the exchange was murdering Anna's self-esteem, slowing killing her pride and her dignity.

Just as she was about to back away from the door with thoughts of entering the building through another door, Derrick glanced her way. How she wished the earth would just open up and swallow her whole!

The huge grin Derrick had directed at Mr. Styes waned, diminishing to a small smile that looked forced, literally plastered on his mouth. The principal turned to look at her also.

She felt like an interloper who was caught in the act

of spying. There was no getting around speaking to Derrick now.

Feeling as though she were walking the slow, agonizing trail toward the guillotine, Anna pulled open the heavy door and went inside.

"Miss Maxwell." Mr. Styes nodded a morning greeting. Then he turned to Derrick. "It's been nice talking to you, Mr. Cheney," he said. "I'll be looking forward to seeing you next week."

Derrick reached out and shook the man's hand.

Then the strangest thing happened. Anna thought she saw Mr. Styes wink at Derrick.

"Good luck today," Mr. Styes said. Then he turned on his heel and walked away.

Anna frowned. Her completely natural curiosity forced her to ask, "What was that all about?"

"Oh...well..." Derrick hedged, "um...Mr. Styes invited me to join the monthly meeting of the room mothers—" then he quickly corrected "—room parents."

"Oh."

She felt as though she was missing something here, that Derrick wasn't telling her everything.

"But...what are you doing here at seven forty-five in the morning?" she asked. "Is there a problem with Timmy?"

The mention of his godson brought a grimace to his face.

"No," he admitted, "Timmy's fine. Although I am feeling a little guilty. You see, I wanted to get here early so I could talk to you, and that left Tim to get on the bus by himself. I know he's fully capable, and there are other mothers on the street who wait at the bus stop—'' he shrugged ''—but I'm still feeling a little guilty.''

Anna only half heard what he'd said. She felt as though she were being smothered by the thick cloak of panic that had enshrouded her when he'd said he'd come to the school to talk to her.

''There's really nothing left to say between us, Derrick.'' Her words were tight and full to bursting with suppressed emotion.

''Sure there is,'' Derrick told her gently. ''Talk to me, Anna. Please.''

''Derrick, the busses will be arriving in five or ten minutes,'' she said, her alarm and agitation growing toward blatant hysteria.

He reached out and touched her sleeve. ''Then give me five or ten minutes.'' He paused, then said, ''Anna, I really want to understand. Help me to understand.''

Instantly she knew what he was asking. He wanted details on her condition. He wanted to know the scientific facts behind her inability to bear children. It was only natural, she decided, that someone as analytical as Derrick would want to know.

''Okay,'' she said. Then she indicated the tiny alcove off the vestibule. ''Let's sit down.''

He waited for her to set her canvas bag down on the tiled floor and sit, before sitting down next to her.

She looked off into the far corner of the alcove, feeling almost comfortable with the task that lay before her, yet unable to look him in the eye as she performed it. ''My condition,'' she began softly, ''is called endometriosis. My doctor uses terms such as 'displaced uterine tissue,' 'cysts,' 'pelvic adhesions,' 'chemical irritation' and 'lesions' to describe it. But the bottom line is that the lesions—'' she did look at him now, feeling he needed to really understand what she was saying "—are…alteration of tissue. It's like…scarring. And it makes it absolutely impossible for me to have children." Her chin dipped a tiny fraction, although she held his gaze steady. "The doctor wasn't able to explain why fate chose me. I'm just one of the unlucky women who have this condition. And there's nothing that can change it. Nothing."

Derrick sat quiet for a moment. Then he slid forward until he was sitting on the edge of the couch.

"Okay," he said. "I think I understand now."

She watched his throat convulse as he swallowed, and even though she was feeling engulfed by a cloud of depression, she couldn't help thinking how the small movement of his neck muscles was deliciously sexy.

Stop it! she commanded herself. *Stop torturing yourself!*

"But what if I were to tell you," he said, his voice whisper soft, "that you could have kids. That *we* could have kids."

"Oh, Derrick." Her mouth pulled into a frown. "Please don't do this. I just told you, it's impossible."

The front door of the school opened, and the first children began to arrive. She could discern the faint smell of bus exhaust as the boys and girls rushed past her.

"I have to go," she said, recklessly grasping any excuse that might keep her from hearing what Derrick had to say.

"Please, Anna. Give me one more minute."

There was something deep, something frantic, in his voice that made her focus her eyes on him.

"I have a kid, Anna," he said. "A kid I love with

all my heart. Timmy's not of my body, but I love him with every cell of my being.''

Anna felt her hands begin to tremble.

"Adoption," he said.

The single word hung between them. She could think of no way to respond. So she simply didn't.

"It's the answer, Anna," he said. "Adoption is the answer to our problem."

Anna wanted desperately to slide into his lap. To hug him and kiss every inch of his handsome face. The fact that he'd worried over her problem—and it was *her* problem, her problem alone—told her a lot about how he felt about her.

But she couldn't do that to him. She couldn't allow him to settle for a less-than-perfect life. He deserved more. He deserved to have it all.

She, too, slid to the edge of the couch. Placing her palms over his hands, she gazed intently at him. "Listen to me, Derrick. I appreciate all that you've said. But I can't let you...I can't let this happen. I have to look ahead. The here and now might look very rosy. But the future would be full of bitterness and regret.'' She shook her head. "I don't want that for you. Or for me.''

His face lifted and tilted a little to one side. "I want to ask you a—''

"Hey, Dad," Timmy called out to Derrick as he entered the school, with his best friend Eric close on his heels.

"Hi, pal." Derrick smiled and waved.

Timmy passed them and went down the hall toward the classrooms.

"Derrick," Anna said, "he called you Dad."

"Yeah, he did."

She nearly smiled at his wide, proud grin.

"He asked me if he could," he went on. Then he shrugged. "I told him I'd love it if he called me Dad."

"That's wonderful," Anna said. "Things will be great between the two of you now."

She started to draw back away from him, but he took her hands in his.

"Can things be great for us now, too?" he asked. "Anna—" he squeezed her hand slightly "—will you marry me?"

"Derrick!" His name came out in a breathless gasp. "Don't," she said in a painful, croaking whisper. "I have to go." She stood up and snatched her bag from the floor. "I have to go, now!"

Blinding panic chased her down the hall as she rushed toward her classroom. Dear God, she had to get away!

She'd anticipated, expected, *wanted* to hear the normal, loud frenzy of her students. She knew the daily ritual would help to calm her frayed nerves. But when she went through the door, the children were seated at their desks, quiet as little mice.

What the heck was going on? she wondered.

Then she saw it. The blackboards were covered with writing.

"Will you marry me, Miss Maxwell?"

The question was repeated nearly a hundred times, she guessed, on the three large blackboards secured to the walls of her room.

"Oh, my," she said. "Oh…my."

"So what do you say, Miss Maxwell?"

She spun around at the sound of Derrick's sexy, oh-so-confident voice.

"Oh, my."

Derrick chuckled, and she was vaguely aware of some twitters from her boys and girls.

"Do it, Miss Maxwell."

She didn't know which little voice that bit of encouragement had come from.

"Yeah, do it," another child said.

"I could use a mom."

Anna's gaze whipped toward Timmy, his beaming face bringing tears to her eyes. She looked at Derrick.

"What about all the things I just said?" she asked him.

He shrugged one shoulder. "They change nothing."

Glancing from one blackboard to another, Anna realized that Derrick must really love her to go to the trouble of doing something so stupid, so romantic, as to propose—a hundred times! She also understood now that he hadn't come to the school to talk about her condition, that he'd planned to ask her to marry him regardless of her medical history.

Derrick loved her. And he was willing to accept her just as she was. With his heart—and his eyes—wide open.

With tears splintering her vision into a dozen shards of brilliant light, she smiled at Derrick. "I love you, Derrick Cheney. And I'd love to marry you."

They rushed toward each other, and as the children cheered, Derrick took her in his arms. She felt so overwhelmed, she simply couldn't stop the tears from falling.

Derrick cradled her face between his hands and planted a light and gentle kiss on her lips. "I love you," he whispered.

The boys and girls really hooted and hollered at the sight.

Anna's throat was closed off with deep emotion, so she simply hung on to the man she loved.

Just then April and Billy came into the classroom.

"What's goin' on?" Billy demanded.

April looked around at her classmates. "What did we miss?"

The whole class laughed—until the school principal entered, then a pin could have been heard hitting the floor, so abruptly silent were the wide-eyed children.

Mr. Styes took in the situation. Anna felt the urge to step out of Derrick's arms, but he held her fast. She sniffed and wiped at her tears.

"I can explain," she said.

"There's no need," the man said. Then he grinned. "Why don't you take the day off?"

"I beg your pardon?" she said.

"Well, it's not every day that a woman gets engaged in such a—" he looked around the room "—*flamboyant* manner." He laughed in spite of himself. "But then, Miss Maxwell, I wouldn't expect anything less from you."

The principal motioned toward the door. "Go ahead," he told Anna and Derrick. "I've called a substitute, and I don't mind staying with your class until she arrives."

"Thanks, Mr. Styes," Derrick said brightly. "Thank you very much."

"But...but..." Anna continued to object weakly as Derrick pulled her out the door and down the hallway.

As soon as they exited the building, Derrick grabbed her around the waist and spun her round and round, burying his face in her loose, flowing hair.

"I love you," he said, nearly shouting the words.

Anna laughed. "And I love you."

The kiss they shared was long and lingeringly sensual. Anna felt a tingling sensation start at the tips of her fingers and travel the length of her body to her toes.

She pulled back and gazed into his dark, glittering eyes.

"So, where are we going?" she asked.

His gaze turned suddenly wicked. "I think our first stop should be the park behind Main Street. At this time of the morning we should have the place all to ourselves."

With their hands clasped in a tight, possessive grip, they ran toward his car, laughing, as Anna's colorful, gauzy skirt whipped behind her in the cool, autumn breeze.

Epilogue

Derrick looked out at the bay where a now teenaged Tim slowly steered a jet ski, giving his eight-year-old "sister" a ride. Little Heather had been a lively ball of energy since the first day she'd come into their home.

"Daddy! Daddy!" he heard his daughter shout from the water. "Look at me! Look at me!"

Waving at Heather and Tim, Derrick smiled. The love he felt for those two children made his heart lurch in his chest.

"Here I come, ready or not."

The small voice coming from behind him had him turning to face the house. Derrick forced himself to remain still as he watched his other daughter make her way down the grassy slope toward him.

The metal brace on six-year-old Susanne's leg made her journey slow and awkward. But over the years, Derrick had come to realize how important it was to the child that he let her walk down the incline all by herself. Susanne's determination and independence never failed to make Derrick feel proud.

"Hey, pumpkin," he said as she hugged onto his leg. "Ready for your swimming lesson?"

"I can't wait!"

He looked expectantly up toward the house.

"Where's your mom?" he asked Susanne.

"She's changin' Samuel's diaper," the little girl told him. "I know he's just a baby and he doesn't know any better, but, boy, he really smelled bad."

Derrick laughed and ruffled the child's baby-fine, blond hair. "Babies do that sometimes."

Samuel was his and Anna's first infant adoption. The two girls had been several years old when they had joined the family. And Derrick couldn't believe how Anna's motherly instinct had blossomed in the past three days since bringing the baby home. He had to admit that he found this soft, gentle side of Anna to be extremely sexy.

"Daddy."

Derrick turned his head toward the sound of his beautiful wife's breathy voice. "Hi, there," he said.

She smiled, and he felt a tightening way down low in his gut. God, how he wanted her. But that would have to wait until later. When the kids were all tucked into bed, and he and Anna had some time all to themselves.

"Our boy's all fed and changed," Anna said. "He's ready for a nap, so I thought I'd cuddle him out here under a tree and watch you and Susanne with your first lesson."

Susanne tugged at the leg of his swimming trunks. "Come on, Daddy. Come on." She twirled one lock of her hair. "I really am glad you're teachin' me to swim,'' she said. ''I hate when Tim makes fun of me for not knowin' how.''

''Well, let me tell you,'' Derrick said, ''there was a time when Tim couldn't swim, either.'' He lowered his voice conspiratorially, ''Not only that, but Tim was afraid of the water.''

The little girl giggled. ''Tim was a scaredy-cat. Tim was a scaredy-cat,'' she sang.

''Now, look what you've done,'' Anna commented.

Derrick grinned. ''It's only right that Susanne have some ammunition to use against her big brother.''

They watched the child make her way down to the water's edge, sit down and begin unfastening her leg brace.

Focusing his attention on his newest son, Derrick bent down and nuzzled the infant's silky soft cheek.

''He smells like heaven,'' he told Anna, straightening and putting his arm around her, drawing her close.

Anna grinned. ''You should have had a whiff of him a few minutes ago.''

Derrick ignored her teasing comment, determined that she wouldn't break this rare moment of romance. ''You smell like heaven, too.''

He tugged aside the strap of her bright purple silk tank top and kissed her bare shoulder. ''Your skin is as soft as Samuel's is, too.''

''Well, thank you, sir.'' Anna smiled.

They stood staring out at the bay, watching their children frolic in the water.

''Did you ever think we'd be this happy?'' he asked her.

''After that disastrous wedding day,'' she said, grimacing, ''I thought we were doomed.''

''Aw, now—'' he hugged her against his side, being

careful of the baby ''—our anniversary was days ago. Once a year, you dwell on our bad beginning. It really wasn't all that bad, was it?''

Anna rolled her eyes. ''Puh…leeze,'' she said.

He had to laugh, the sudden burst of sound frightening the baby. ''Yeah,'' he finally admitted, ''you're right. But we did turn out all right.''

She crooned to the baby a moment. ''Yes,'' she said, kissing Derrick softly on the cheek, ''we did turn out all right, didn't we?''

He bent just enough so he could whisper in her ear, describing in great detail all the ways in which he planned on proving his love late in the night when the two of them would be alone.

''You know,'' she said, her voice husky with desire, ''it's bad luck to make promises and then break them.''

He gazed deeply into sea green eyes—eyes that had captured his heart from the very first. ''I wouldn't dare,'' he told her. Then he grinned. ''It's too much fun fulfilling them.''

Derrick kissed Anna soundly on the mouth, a kiss that left no question as to how very much he loved her, and then he trotted to the water to teach his daughter to swim.

*   *   *   *   *

Wondering what happened to the other bachelors in THE SINGLE DADDY CLUB? *Don't miss* NANNY IN THE NICK OF TIME, *coming next month from Silhouette Romance.*

Silhouette Romance proudly invites you
to get to know the members of

The Single
Daddy Club

a new miniseries by award-winning author
Donna Clayton

Derrick: Ex-military man who unexpectedly
falls into fatherhood
MISS MAXWELL BECOMES A MOM (March '97)

Jason: Widowed daddy desperately in need of some live-in help
NANNY IN THE NICK OF TIME (April '97)

Reece: Single and satisfied father of one about
to meet his Ms. Right
BEAUTY AND THE BACHELOR DAD (May '97)

Don't miss any of these heartwarming stories as
three single dads say bye-bye to their bachelor days.
Only from

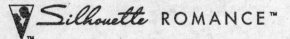

Silhouette ROMANCE™

Take 4 bestselling love stories FREE

Plus get a FREE surprise gift!

As seen on TV!
Free Gift Offer

With a Free Gift proof-of-purchase from any Silhouette® book,
you can receive a beautiful cubic zirconia pendant.

This gorgeous marquise-shaped stone is a genuine cubic
zirconia—accented by an 18" gold tone necklace.

(Approximate retail value $19.95)

Send for yours today...
compliments of ▼ *Silhouette*®
TM

To receive your free gift, a cubic zirconia pendant, send us one original proof-of-
purchase, photocopies not accepted, from the back of any Silhouette Romance™,
Silhouette Desire®, Silhouette Special Edition®, Silhouette Intimate Moments®
or Silhouette Yours Truly™ title available in February, March and April at your favorite
retail outlet, together with the Free Gift Certificate, plus a check or money order for
$1.65 U.S./$2.15 CAN. (do not send cash) to cover postage and handling, payable
to Silhouette Free Gift Offer. We will send you the specified gift. Allow 6 to 8 weeks for
delivery. Offer good until April 30, 1997 or while quantities last. Offer valid in the
U.S. and Canada only.

Free Gift Certificate

Name: _____

Address: _____

City: _____ State/Province: _____ Zip/Postal Code: _____

Mail this certificate, one proof-of-purchase and a check or money order for postage
and handling to: SILHOUETTE FREE GIFT OFFER 1997. In the U.S.: 3010 Walden
Avenue, P.O. Box 9077, Buffalo NY 14269-9077. In Canada: P.O. Box 613, Fort Erie,
Ontario L2Z 5X3.

FREE GIFT OFFER
ONE PROOF-OF-PURCHASE

084-KFD

To collect your fabulous FREE GIFT, a cubic zirconia pendant, you must include this
original proof-of-purchase for each gift with the properly completed Free Gift Certificate.

084-KFD

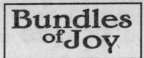

Bundles of JOY

The biggest romantic surprises come in the smallest packages!

January:

HAVING GABRIEL'S BABY by Kristin Morgan (#1199)

After one night of passion Joelle was expecting! The dad-to-be, rancher Gabriel Lafleur, insisted on marriage. But could they find true love as a family?

April:

YOUR BABY OR MINE? by Marie Ferrarella (#1216)

Single daddy Alec Beckett needed help with his infant daughter! When the lovely Marissa Rogers took the job with an infant of her own, Alec realized he wanted this mom-for-hire *permanently*—as part of a real family!

Don't miss these irresistible Bundles of Joy,
coming to you in January and April,
only from

You're About to Become a *Privileged Woman*

Reap the rewards of fabulous free gifts and benefits with proofs-of-purchase from Silhouette and Harlequin books

Pages & Privileges™

It's our way of thanking you for buying our books at your favorite retail stores.

PROOF OF PURCHASE
SR-PP23
Offer expires March 31, 1997

Pages & Privileges ™

**Harlequin and Silhouette—
the most privileged readers in the world!**

For more information about Harlequin and Silhouette's PAGES & PRIVILEGES program call the Pages & Privileges Benefits Desk: 1-503-794-2499

Silhouette® ™